MIRACLES ON MAPLE HILL

by the same author

CURIOUS MISSIE

PLAIN GIRL

AWARDED THE 1957 NEWBERY MEDAL
*"For the most distinguished contribution
to American literature for children"*

HARCOURT, BRACE & WORLD, IN

VIRGINIA SORENSEN

MIRACLES ON MAPLE HILL

ILLUSTRATED BY BETH AND JOE KRUSH

EW YORK

LIBRARY OF CONGRESS CATALOG CARD NUMBER: 56-8358

PRINTED IN THE UNITED STATES OF AMERICA

CONTENTS

CONTENTS

MIRACLES ON MAPLE HILL

1 THERE'S ALL OUTDOORS

"Mother, say the scoot-thing again," Marly said.

She slid forward in the car seat, talking right against her mother's neck, over her coat collar. "Say it just the way your grandma said it."

"Marly—*again?*" Mother asked. "And please don't breathe down my neck, dear!" She was driving, and the road was narrow and snowy and worrisome.

"Just say it *once* more. The way she said it."

Marly noticed the look Mother gave Daddy who sat beside her in the front seat. She could tell that Mother was afraid Daddy would object to hearing the same thing over and over. He was more tired than usual, even. When he asked Mother to drive, he was always as tired as he could be. Now he sat with his eyes closed and his chin buried in the collar of his jacket.

But it was for him, really, that Marly wanted Mother to say the scoot-thing again. Maybe they didn't think she knew why they were going to Maple Hill. But she did.

"Just once. I promise never to ask again. I *promise,*" Marly said.

Her brother Joe turned from the window for a change. The whole way up from Pittsburgh he'd kept his face glued

3

to it like an old fly. "Why don't you just say it to yourself?" he asked. "Mother's said it ten hundred times."

"I want *her* to say it—just once."

If Joe asked her why she wanted Mother to say it, Marly couldn't have told him. The truth was that when Mother said those certain words all the good feelings came back. Grandma's whole house and yard and her whole Maple Hill were in those words, just the way Mother had described them ever since Marly could remember. Grandma was in them, too, with the way Mother said her voice was, like a bird's voice if it pretended to be cross but really wasn't. Mother was in them, too, but in a special way. Not the way she was now, but the way she had been when she was Marly's age. Every summer she had come to visit her Grandma at Maple Hill, right here in Pennsylvania's corner.

How so many things could be in a few words was something else Marly didn't know. But it was the same way the whole feel of school can be in the sound of a bell ringing. Or the way the whole feeling of spring can be in one robin on a fence post.

Daddy opened his eyes. "You might as well say it, Lee, and get it over with," he said. He did not look at Mother or at Marly or at anybody. He liked to do the driving himself, especially v   a road was as bad as this. But he was too tired. Soon   he had come home, while people were still marveling that he had come b ck at all after being a soldier and a prisone and everything, Marly had heard him say to Mother, "I think I'm going to be tired forever."

But Mother had answered, "Of course you won't. You know, Dale, I've been thinking—we could go up to that old place of Grandma's, Maple Hill. What you need is all outdoors for a while."

"Honestly, Marly, I don't *see*—" Mother began. But she sighed, and then she said it. For a long time when Marly was little, she had corrected Mother every time any one of the words was the least bit different, so now Mother always said it exactly right. Every syllable. Every other word had to come strong, as in a nursery rhyme:

"Now *scoot*, you *two*, for *goodness' sakes!* Up *here*, there's *all* out*doors!*"

There! Marly sat back again. If there was all outdoors, there couldn't be very much indoors where all the trouble was. She could see the little old woman in a blue dress and a white apron, with her broom in her hand. She was pretending to sweep the children out, as Mother said, because they kept hanging around the house after they arrived. The first time Mother told about it, a long time ago, Marly had asked, "Why did you hang around? Why didn't you go outside and play?" Mother laughed and said, "Grandma thought it was because we were too used to being penned up in town. We were so used to having walls around us and ceilings over us that the sky and the country scared us to death. Grandma hated cities. We could hardly ever get her to come for a visit. She insisted that my brother and I come every summer, out to Maple Hill. She told us, 'The only place worth a grain of salt is where a child can go out and run as he pleases.'"

All outdoors! Marly stared out of the window on her side as Joe did on his.

Maybe, she thought, it wasn't just because of the city. She could remember times that had been nice there, and happy, before Daddy ever went away. And even while he was gone, sometimes. Mother paid a lot of attention, and they went to the museum on Sunday afternoons and to hear the Pittsburgh Symphony and for picnics in the park. Everybody felt sorry for Mother because Daddy was missing, and nobody expected he would ever come back. But then he came.

She wouldn't even think it was better before Daddy came back. Nobody must think such a terrible thing. But it was a worry. If a door slammed behind you, for instance, he'd shout, *"Who slammed that door?"* You'd start to tell him the wind made it slam, but there wasn't time. Mother always hurried in, saying, "Sssssssh! Sssssssh! Sssssssh!"

Everything would be better in all outdoors. Mother expected it would be and it would. Already things looked better. For two hours the most wonderful outdoors, all hills and snow and big tall trees and farmhouses, had been going past the windows. Once in a while it was interrupted by a pretty little town, and then it began again.

"Marly," Mother said anxiously, half turning her head but watching the road at the same time, "you mustn't expect it to be exactly the way I said. Grandma's been gone from Maple Hill for nearly twenty years. Uncle John's lived here off and on, but . . . Well, it's an old run-down place. Not like these lovely farms on the road at all."

"I know *that*," Marly said. "But we're going to fix it up."

Those were the words Mother used when Marly first heard them talking about it. Daddy had jumped the way he did sometimes and said, "You mean it's going to fix *me* up!"

"Dale, I didn't say that."

"You meant it."

"Well, all right then," Mother had said, going red in the face. "Why shouldn't we say it right out? I'm hoping it will."

That had been just a little while ago, during the Christmas holidays. You expected everything to be wonderful at Christmas time, and the town was wonderful, with colored lights and decorated trees in every direction. Marvelous things were piled in every window along the streets downtown, and big organ music made the sidewalks sort of tremble. But this year something had gone wrong with everything. Daddy didn't even come from his room Christmas morning to see the presents. Mother had explained, trying to smile. He was tired and hurt and not really cross. He was sick and discouraged, not angry at them or at anybody. There was a lot of difference, Mother said.

Of course it was true. But the house felt ugly and tight. Joe went off with his crowd right after breakfast. During the holidays he found someplace to go every day.

Once when they began to talk about coming to Maple Hill, Daddy had said, "I don't know whether I can do it, Lee. All that wood to cut and everything. Do you think I can swing an ax any more?"

"Why, of course," Mother said. "And Joe can help. He's twelve, isn't he? That's just the age Grandma used to say kids stopped being a nuisance and started being useful."

In two years I'll be twelve, too! Marly had thought. She was so interested in imagining the piles and piles of kindlings she would cut that she forgot to listen to what Mother and Daddy said next. She was reaching up in her mind to put a piece of wood on a pile higher than her head. But then Mother said something so interesting and wonderful she couldn't help hearing it. "When I was a little girl up at Grandma's," Mother said, "I was certain that Maple Hill was the place where all the miracles had happened."

Daddy didn't laugh. For a minute it was as if the two

7

of them were holding their breath together. Then Daddy said, "I'm afraid miracles don't happen any more—even at Maple Hill."

"We'll go find out," Mother said.

That was soon after Christmas. Now it was March, and here they were, going to find out.

"It's not very far from here," Mother said.

Now all outdoors seemed to be mostly trees close along the road. There were bare limbs that bent against the car, scraping as it passed, brushing off their snow. Hemlocks were like frosted green. Mother shifted gears, and the car was a big black noise in the middle of a huge white quietness.

"What a hill!" Mother said. "I'm not even sure this car is going to make it."

They all leaned forward as if that might help somehow. The car was really struggling. "I've heard stories about these spring roads!" Mother said, pretending not to mind. "But it was always summer when I came, and I never believed them."

The car stood still, then, its wheels singing and whirling. Marly saw Daddy's face set hard, the way it always did when he was angry or upset. His cheeks sank in, and she could see his heart beating in his neck. Mother stepped on the gas, and the wheels sang still louder and the engine roared like a truck.

"Shall I get out and push?" Joe asked eagerly.

"That's all we need," Daddy said in an angry voice. "Just Joe to get out and push!"

Joe's face went red. Daddy's was white. Mother roared the engine louder and louder.

"Stop it, Lee. You'll only spin the wheels," Daddy said.

8

When the sound of the car died, silence was suddenly everywhere. It seemed coming and going in every direction, and they were in the middle of it. The front of the car tipped upward on the bare beginning of the long hill.

"It can't be far to Chris's place now," Mother said. "They can probably pull us out. People here are used to such things."

"We didn't even think to get chains," Daddy said. "What farmers we'll be!"

"Mother—" Marly began, but Joe interrupted her. He said just what she'd meant to say, except that he said "I" and she had meant to say "we."

"Mother, I'll get my boots on and go ahead and tell 'em," Joe said.

"I'll go too," Marly said.

Joe looked at her in a superior way. "You'd just slow me down," he said. That was the way he talked to her lately, even when it wasn't true. She never could say it wasn't true, though, because every time it made an argument and Daddy thought every argument was a fight and had to be stopped instantly. He said there was plenty of fighting going on in the world without them doing any of it.

Mother hesitated. "I don't know what else—" She looked at Daddy.

"My boots are in the trunk," Joe said, and out he went.

"Mine are too. Get mine too!" Marly cried.

"He'll be sopping wet before he even gets his boots on," Mother said. "Who would have thought there'd still be snow like this up here?" Her voice was worried. Daddy didn't say one word. He just sat still, staring out of the windshield up the long hill.

"Mother—Daddy—can't I go too? Joe knows I can go as fast as he can! He knows I can!" Marly cried.

"Hush now," Mother said. "There's no use both of you catching your death of cold."

"Mother, we wouldn't—"

"Don't argue, Marly! Please!" Mother said. She gave Marly the look that said: *Now don't talk about it any more or you'll worry Daddy again.*

"*Please!*"

"Marly! You heard what I said!"

"But, Mother—"

"Marly, don't argue!" Daddy's voice was fierce.

Joe scrambled back in the car with his boots and pulled them on, jamming his jeans inside. How important he acted! You'd have thought he was the President of the United States or something. For a minute Marly hated him. If he just said he'd like her to go along, she could. But he wouldn't say it for the world. She always said she'd like him to go along wherever she was going, and it was even true. But he'd never say it. Never, never, never.

"Please, Joe," she whispered so Daddy and Mother wouldn't hear.

But Joe didn't seem to hear her either. Mother said, "Joe, you'll likely see the Chris place as soon as you get to the top of the hill. It's a big white house down a lane. Green shutters. Behind it is a huge red barn. I'm pretty sure it's the next place—" Her voice didn't sound sure at all.

"Just tell whoever *is* at the next place," Daddy said.

"I hope I'm right," Mother said. "They're such wonderful people and were such good friends to Grandma—and to John and me."

Joe got out. He acted more important than ever, pulling

10

his gloves tight up over his sleeves. Marly said once more, "Mother—" but Mother looked at her, hard. Joe started out, turning to smile and wave. Marly hated him again, this time even more, but in a minute he was walking alone up the hill—littler—and littler—and the three sat silently, watching him. By the time he got to the top of the hill she loved him again and opened the door and hopped out on the running board to wave. He waved back. His hat looked very red and small, a dot on the white road, against the sky.

"For heaven's sake, close the door. No use freezing while we wait," Daddy said.

But Marly hardly heard. "I smell smoke," she said. "Look—look! right there!"

Only a little distance up the hill, on the side where she stood, was a wreath of blue smoke winding into the air. It looked lovely, curling upward from the trees.

"Mother, may I go and see? May I?" she cried.

Mother and Daddy looked at each other. They both looked up the hill where Joe had disappeared.

"I can see a tiny little road. It turns in there—see, behind us. We didn't even notice it before."

"It can't do any harm, can it? While we're waiting? Then she won't—" Mother stopped. She almost said: Then she won't be making a noise and fussing and being in the way.

Marly saw their looks saying "why not?" and scrambled out for her own boots, using the tramped places Joe had made. Now it was her turn to start out, to turn and wave from the little road, to follow the deep ruts.

"Don't go far! Come right back!" Mother called.

"It's got horse tracks!" Marly cried back. "And tractor tracks!"

Then the road turned into the trees.

How beautiful, how beautiful! The land went up and down, with snow everywhere, unbroken except where the little road wound through. But then there was another little road, going into the trees. And another. She stood still, wondering. The tracks went around—over there and over there—in a big circle, and . . . She stood staring. Every tree was hanging with bright buckets. And every bucket had a little pointed lid, like a cap. Once she had seen a picture in a book at school—

Then she heard somebody ahead, chopping wood. The sound of the ax coming down was sharp and clear. And there he was, the woodchopper, swinging up and swinging down again. The sound of the ax hitting the wood reached Marly as he lifted it up again. He stood by an immense pile of wood, and behind the pile was a little brown house. It had a high brown smokestack that the blue smoke was pouring from and an extra little roof that seemed to be sitting on great billowing white clouds of steam.

She glanced back toward the road. It was as if another step would bring the ordinary world completely to an end and this would be Wonderland. Even the sights and sounds didn't match here. Near her a bucket hung against a tree, and she distinctly heard a sound of drip—drip—drip—

The man saw her as she came. He stopped chopping and lifted a hand to wave. He was smiling. Then, suddenly, he dropped the ax and began to walk toward her. She didn't know whether to go on walking herself or turn and run. But she went on walking, and as he came closer he cried

12

suddenly, "Lee! For goodness' sakes! Lee!"

She could smell the smoke on his overalls when he held out his hand. He smelled wonderful, like a smoked ham. His face was round and red and fresh, and he was absolutely huge all over. His hand closed over hers, and his laugh was as big as he was in his huge blue jeans and sweater.

"Imagine me calling you Lee!" he said. "You must be her girl Marly. But you're your mother all over again. I'm Mr. Chris."

Before she had time to say anything—about the car or the hill or the trouble or anything else—he laughed and said, "Can you smell that, Marly? Did you get that whiff just then from the sugarhouse? I told my wife this morning, this time Lee's coming for the first breath of spring."

She had got it. It was absolute sweetness, like a drift of scent from a lilac bush. Like passing an orchard in full bloom. But different. A different sweetness—

"Your great-grandma used to say there was all outdoors in that smell," Mr. Chris said. "She called it the first miracle when the sap came up."

She looked up at him in surprise. So that's where Mother had got the idea of the miracles.

"Where are your folks? At the house?" he asked.

In two minutes they were on the way to the rescue. There were two big horses that he used to gather sap from trees on the steep hills where a tractor would go head-over-wheels, he said. But the tractor was the thing to take that car home in a hurry. Marly sat beside him. The tractor was bright orange against the snow. She felt like a queen in a high chariot as they rolled off along the little road among the trees.

2 MEET MR. CHRIS

Marly knew it was sad for Joe, but she couldn't help being pleased by the flabbergasted look on his face. He was just plowing his way past the mailbox saying *J. Chris* when they came along behind him. She was still riding high on the tractor with Mr. Chris, and the car came along behind like a good little poodle on a chain.

"I found Mr. Chris!" she called to Joe. "I saw the smoke and found Mr. Chris!"

She knew Daddy would be disgusted at her for bragging, but after all Joe had to be told, didn't he? He stood with his eyes sticking out like a snail's.

"And you're Joe," Mr. Chris said. He leaned down and took Joe's shoulder in his big hand and shook him the way you shake somebody you love and are glad to see. "How'd you get up that hill so fast? I told your mother nobody'd make it today without snowshoes."

Joe smiled and felt better again right away. Mr. Chris was a man who wanted everybody to feel all right. Marly felt a tickle of shame about bragging to make Joe feel bad—but she hoped Joe felt a tickle of shame too for leaving her behind.

If he did, it didn't show. He jumped onto the tractor and nearly pushed her off.

"Careful there. Room for everybody," Mr. Chris said.

They rolled down the lane to the big house. A lady came out on the porch with her arms folded in her apron to keep warm. She had the most beautiful white hair Marly had ever seen. Great Grandma must have looked like that whenever Mother came for a visit to Maple Hill, Marly thought. But this was Mrs. Chris.

"Chrissie, they're here!" Mr. Chris called. "You know what—I had to get them up that hill, just like you said I would."

You would have thought Mr. Chris and Chrissie were real relations and not just neighbors that Mother used to know. Everybody was hugging and kissing and crying out each others' names. "Lee! How wonderful . . . Why, you've hardly changed. Surely this isn't Marly. And Joe. But I've still been thinking they were babies . . ."

Daddy stood back of it, alone, the way he usually did at home when friends came to call. But Mother, as always, turned to find him. "Chrissie—this is Dale," she said.

Her voice was even more special when she said, "This is Dale," than it was when she said, "This is Marly," or "This is Joe." Marly loved the voice and the look that seemed to say: *Isn't he wonderful? And isn't it wonderful he is here when he was gone so long and everybody thought he might never come home again?*

Mrs. Chris kissed Daddy and then stood back with her hands on his shoulders, looking at him. "You look like your picture, except you're not as thin as you were. I cut it out of the newspaper, and it's posted on my kitchen wall."

Daddy stood rather stiffly, the way he always did when people talked about what a hero he was and how much they'd heard about him.

Mother said, "You know, Chrissie, I've never been here in sugaring season before? I always wanted to, I remember, and Grandma was always insisting. But we could never get here until school was out."

"We've had a month of it already," Mr. Chris said. "The best season I've seen in years. Chrissie and I were saying, all of you ought to come to the camp tonight."

"Mother, let's!" Marly cried. "Joe, there's a little brown house—"

"I know what a sugar camp is," Joe said.

"You must eat before you go on to Maple Hill," Chrissie said. "Lee, I sent our man Fritz over to kindle a fire. I thought going in there in the cold—" She looked at Mother with a frown that didn't seem to suit her face at all. "There wasn't much I could do to straighten up, Lee," she said. "If you'd let me know sooner—" She began bustling around the huge warm kitchen, which had a stove twice the size of an ordinary stove and a table ten feet long.

"I wrote late on purpose so you wouldn't bother," Mother said.

Marly looked with dismay at the table being set. She slipped close to Mother and whispered, "Do we have to

18

stay and eat here?" She could hardly wait to go on and see Maple Hill.

"Hush," Mother said, and blushed.

"Why do we?" Joe whispered. This time he and Marly were on the same side. "All that lunch we brought—"

Daddy heard. "You two sit down and behave yourselves," he said. "Do as your Mother says."

The whole day would go, just visiting, and they had to leave again tomorrow. As nice as Mr. Chris and Chrissie were, nothing could seem right or finished until they had got to Maple Hill. Getting there had taken weeks of talk and worry already; it was slower than Christmas. Now it was so close—"only a little piece down the road from Chris's" as Mother always said—and they still couldn't see it.

"I'm not hungry at all. Maybe Joe and me could just—"

"Now, hush!" Mother said again.

But Mrs. Chris had heard. She looked at Marly, smiling. "There's not a bit of use you being starved when you get there," she said. "Your mother'll have plenty else to do without worrying about feeding the family the first five minutes."

Mr. Chris had to get back to the sugar camp to watch his fire. "Mother, can't we go back with him?" Marly asked. That would be second best.

"Later. Maybe tomorrow," Mother said, and gave Marly a look that said, "What a bother you are . . ."

So they watched Mr. Chris go off in the bright chariot, out along the lane and down the road and over the hill, where he disappeared as if he had fallen off the earth.

"It's wonderful, Joe. Hundreds of trees with buckets hanging around them like charm bracelets. And smoke coming out of the little brown house. It looks like the old witch's house in *Hansel and Gretel*."

"I've read all about sugar camps," Joe said. He was still bothered because she'd seen it first, she could tell, and because she had turned out to be the one to come to the rescue.

"But there's a wonderful *smell*," she said. "I'll bet you didn't find that in any old book!"

Actually, eating at Chrissie's was wonderful. When you ate her food, you knew why Mr. Chris had got to be so huge. Mrs. Chris didn't potter around either. Everything was ready in a few minutes because she had expected them. She even knew they were in a big hurry and didn't mind at all.

"Would you like me to go along, Lee? I might be able to help a little," she said. "We've tried to keep track of the place, but an empty house—I don't know. One thing and another seems to go to pieces. Chris wrote you about somebody breaking in—"

"Yes," Mother said. "But we don't mind having to work at it. In fact, that's what we want; it's what we came for. Dale's going to stay on there and work while the children finish school."

"He'd best do some of his eating with us," Mrs. Chris said.

Daddy started to protest.

"What's one more to feed?" Mrs. Chris said with a laugh. "You could do with some fattening, Dale. Anything I love to do is fatten a man."

Daddy's face looked tight. Marly held her breath, remembering something he said to Mother before they started out. "I want to be alone. None of that country good-neighbor business, I hope. Everybody trading dinners and knowing everybody else's business."

Mother noticed too, Marly could tell. She stood up quickly and said, "Well, we'd better be off, I guess. Chrissie, that was so wonderful . . ."

Mrs. Chris stood on the porch again to wave them good-by. "If you should get stuck again, just honk and honk!" she called. "But I don't think you will. Fritz cleared the road this morning."

Marly felt her hands clenched tight with excitement. *Now—soon*—she thought. Joe had his face glued to his window again. "Joe, it's not on that side," she said.

He looked at her. "How do you know?" he asked.

Mother turned with a laugh. "Yes, how did you, Marly? I don't think I ever said. Did I?"

For a minute Marly felt confused. She could see it in her mind, the whole place, the slope, the trees, the tumbly barn against the hill. Then suddenly she knew. "You said you used to sit on the front porch and watch the sun go down," she said.

Mother and Daddy looked at each other, the look that said: What a child! She's quite bright after all! Joe crowded over to look from her window, too. He looked determined and she knew how he felt; after what happened before, he absolutely had to see Maple Hill first. And she decided to let him. Boys were queer. They seemed afraid they'd stop being boys altogether if they couldn't be first at everything.

Suddenly the sun came out. All day it had been hidden, but now it burst from the clouds. Everywhere the crusted snow began to shine like Christmas cotton. It was only a minute, and then it disappeared again beneath a cloud.

And there, as if the blinding moment of brightness had created it like the wave of a wand, was the house on Maple Hill.

She thought Joe would never see it. But suddenly he said, "Is that it? That little house—"

"That's it," Mother said firmly, and turned the car off the road. "I told you it was just a small place, Didn't I?"

"But it's pretty—little and pretty," Marly said quickly. And it was, in a way, though it looked awfully lonely in the vast countryside—and dilapidated too. The porch was heavy with snow and you could see where one step had fallen in. Huge snowy bushes hung over the railing. It looked as if nobody had lived there for a hundred years. The trees on the hill were huge and bare, like skeletons.

"I always loved the windows," Mother said as if she was trying to find something good to say.

They were all little squares, Marly noticed then, with tipsy shutters.

"They're so nice with ruffled white curtains," Mother said.

Everybody sat still. Nobody could think of anything else to say for a minute. Then Daddy spoke. "Fritz seems to have made a good big fire. Look at the smoke coming from the chimney."

"Me go in first!" Joe cried then. "Mother, can I unlock the door?"

"Maybe we'd better flip a nickel for a privilege like that," Daddy said, looking at Marly.

But she shook her head. She sat still while Joe got out and ran to the back door, while Daddy and Mother followed. She wanted time to say something to herself that she had planned to say.

It had to be the right place. All outdoors. With miracles.

Not crowded and people being cross and mean. Daddy not tired all the time any more. Mother not worried. But it looked little and old to be all that. She was afraid, now that she was actually here, that it wasn't. She wished that they were still on the way. Sometimes even Christmas wasn't as much fun as getting ready for it. Maybe thinking about Maple Hill would turn out to be better than Maple Hill itself.

She whispered, "Please, let there be miracles."

"Marly!" Mother called. "Aren't you coming?"

Forever and forever now, on Christmas morning, Marly knew, she would stop on the stairs where she couldn't see the living room yet. Afraid maybe somebody had forgotten to light the tree. Because—that once—it really had happened. She felt afraid to go into this house now, even though she didn't know what she expected inside. She didn't even know what she'd miss if it wasn't there.

"Marly!" Daddy came out of the door again. She heard him say to Mother, "What's wrong with that child? In such a hurry to get here and then just sitting—"

She got out of the car then, saying the words once more, and ran every step of the way. Daddy laughed and opened the door wide for her to go running in.

3 MAPLE HILL

As dusty and musty as that house was, it was full of treasures. All Marly and Joe could do was run around looking and yelling at each other, "Look! Look at this!"

First the kitchen. There was a stove nearly as big as Chrissie's, and water was steaming away in a cunning tub at the side which Mother said was called a "reservoir." "Mother, that's what you used to dip your bath water out of," Marly said. She had imagined how it must be. Now she knew.

"We kept rain water in it," Mother said. "That's what comes from the pump there by the sink. That water's so soft that one rub of the soap makes it full of suds."

It was queer thinking about water being "soft" and "hard," and right away Joe began pumping at the funny old thing that stood between the sink and the cupboard. Nothing happened, and Mother said, "You have to pour some water in the top first, Joe, to prime it."

So he did. Old brown smelly water began coming out, but soon it got paler and paler, and Mother had them empty the reservoir of ordinary water and put rain water in it. "Tonight you can have a bath in that old tub, just like I did—if it doesn't leak," Mother said to Marly.

"Let it leak," Daddy said. "Then we'll automatically have enough suds on the floor to scrub it." He sounded happy and cheerful and interested. He was exploring things too.

The old cupboard wasn't fastened to the wall like in an apartment. It had a sliding door right in the middle, and under the door were all kinds of fascinating things: faded boxes of spices and mustard and herbs and a little grinder full of peppercorns. A bigger grinder had a cute little drawer filled with spiderwebs and ancient coffee—and with mouse-leavings. Everywhere there were mouse-leavings. "You can tell who has been living here!" Mother said.

Daddy and Joe went out to look at the old barn while Marly and Mother looked at the things in the cupboard. "These were Grandma's everyday dishes," Mother said. " 'Heavy so we couldn't break them,' she used to say. There are some good, fine dishes somewhere in a box, Uncle John said."

In the top drawer Marly found dingy, blackened spoons and forks and knives. Mother said, "You see why Mrs. Chris thought we'd better eat where we were. You and I will have to get enough of these cleaned before supper-time."

"First can I see the rest of the house?" Marly asked. Imagine being stuck in the kitchen, no matter how interesting it was!

"Of course," Mother said. "But, Marly—this is the first place we women have to start to *dig*."

We women. Marly felt proud when Mother said that.

They went into the dining room which had a heavy round table and cane-bottomed chairs and a cupboard across one corner. There was a window seat with a long cushion on it that had its stuffing coming out. "I helped make that cushion one summer," Mother said. "It was lovely, bright yellow. Grandma helped me cut it out, just to fit." She touched it, and dust flew out. "It's hard to believe it was bright yellow," she said. She looked around. "I wonder what happened to Grandma's old sewing machine? Uncle John seems to have kept out just the things a *man* uses."

"Where did you eat? Here?" Marly asked.

"On holidays, in here. Mostly in the kitchen."

There was everything to find out. Where did you sleep? Where did you play? Where did Grandma sleep?

Upstairs were three little bedrooms under the eaves. A wonderful old feather tick was rolled up and wrapped in canvas and put away in a huge trunk. Quilts were there, too, the very quilts Mother had told about. Sunbonnet girls. Wedding rings.

"The pillows are here too, wonderful down pillows," Mother said, and searched them out. "How musty they smell! When we come back, we'll hang them out in the sun." She began to sneeze and had to put them quickly away again.

"I knew how everything was going to look," Marly said. It was really true. "Even if you hadn't told me, I'd have known which was your room and which was John's and which was Grandma's. But your window is the best. It looks *out* the most."

"It faces the valley, not the hill. I always liked that," Mother said. "This should be your room, Marly, because it was mine." She came and stood by the window, and never in her whole life had Marly ever loved her quite as

26

much as at that moment. "Sometimes I was a little lonely up here," Mother said. "It's good you'll have Joe to explore with. John never seemed to want me along, and there were lots of boys for him to go with. Hunting and fishing, things like that."

"Joe says I'm too slow. He won't take me either," Marly said. "But I don't care. Sometimes you can go with me, and I'm not a bit afraid to go alone."

Out of the window were wide fields with wonderful rail fences just like in the pictures of Lincoln splitting rails. There were sudden gullies, too, where you knew streams would flow when the snow melted, and in every direction were fringes of brown and green. The woods even came tumbling into the fields where new trees were growing.

"I tried going alone," Mother said, "but I never really liked it. The minute I got into the woods it felt lonely, and I got scared and hurried back to Grandma." She put her hand on Marly's shoulder in a nice friendly way. "I'll try not to be too busy, but a farmer's wife has an awful lot to do." She leaned close to the window and rubbed some of the dust off to see better. "You know, I've never seen it like this before—with snow on it and the leaves gone. It's lovely, isn't it? You see the shapes of things." Her breath made the glass misty, and so did Marly's, so everything had a kind of mysterious fog around it. "If I could draw—" Mother said.

Marly remembered some of the pictures at home and Mother saying, "Yes, I used to draw a lot. But there doesn't seem to be time any more."

"You draw real good pictures, Mother," she said.

Mother laughed and shook her head. "I was just thinking, if I drew what's out of the window now, it'd have to be with pen and ink. In the summer you have to have great big brushes full of green. When we come back in June, you'll see."

Marly hardly heard the last of it. She had opened a dresser drawer—and there was a whole family of wonderful little mice! Seven naked little pink creatures lay all wound up together with closed eyes and ears standing up and long whiskers sticking out and little pointed noses and tiny strings of tails.

"Look! Aren't they beautiful?" she cried.

"Well, we'll have to get rid of *them!*" Mother said, peering in.

"Mother! Why, they're darling—"

"Maybe they're darling now," Mother said briskly, "but they're not living here any more. *We* are."

"Goodness, there's plenty of room for everybody," Marly said.

"Mice are dirty," Mother said, and actually shuddered.

Marly didn't always know when not to argue, but this time she knew. She and Joe had read a story about some children who had mice for pets. She said no more to Mother but thought to herself: I'll talk to Joe and he can find a box. We'll teach these little mice to be as clean as pins—and to do tricks. Then Mother will just see how wrong she was.

"Well, we'd better go down and get busy," Mother said. "We'll go over the whole kitchen first."

When Joe and Daddy came in, they were all excited about the discoveries they had made outside. Daddy's cheeks looked red and his eyes looked brighter than Marly had ever seen them. "There's an old buggy out there, Lee, in perfect condition," Daddy said. "You always said how

29

much you liked riding around in that buggy. Mr. Chris said we could borrow a horse sometimes."

"There's a sleigh too. It's still even got all its plush on," Joe said.

"There are a whole lot of good tools in that workshop against the barn," Daddy said. "Rusted, some of 'em, but mostly pretty good."

"John always loved tools," Mother said. "He was so fussy he wouldn't let anybody else touch his things." She was on the floor by a bucket of suds, wiping the floor, and Marly saw the look on her face. She looked as if she might cry, and Marly thought, "Oh, dear!" But instead Mother only said, "It's amazing how much everything's the same, after all this time. The pattern of this floor . . . my room . . . Dale, there's even a pile of my old letters in one of the dresser drawers, all surrounded with mice." Her voice got brisk. "Joe, there's a whole family of baby mice in a drawer in the first bedroom. You can get rid of them and set all those traps you brought."

Marly trembled. "I'll show Joe where they are," she said.

You'd have thought Mother read her mind. "We are *not* going to keep those baby mice, Marly, and that's that," she said.

"I should say not," Daddy said.

Marly felt them watching her as she started up the narrow little stairs after Joe. They were thinking of all the funny little animals, stray cats and dogs and things, she had always wanted to bring in and keep. She whispered right into Joe's ear: "Joe, they're *darling*. And nobody even needs to know. We can get a box or something and they can live in it. We'll put a lid on, and you can build a house after a while and put a wheel in it for them to run around on—"

"You're thinking of rats," he said. "These are just old house mice."

"*Whisper*," she said. "Because—"

"I won't either whisper," he said. "You heard what Mother said. And it's just silly, that's all. Mice make a mess all over everything and spoil people's books and get in the flour bin and crawl in people's clothes."

"These won't," she said. "I'll take care of them. I'll see that they stay right in the box."

Joe looked at her in disgust. "Do you know how many babies just one of these meadow mice have in a year?" he demanded. "I read in a book—*one thousand babies a year!* Could you keep a thousand mice in any box, or do you want them running all over your room and in and out of your pillowcases and everything. One year and you'd have *seven thousand* mice from that one drawerful!"

"Joe, you're making that up. There never were that many baby mice."

"Weren't there? Well, there were too! I can show you the book when we get back home. It's in my *Natural History Field Book*." Bravely and elaborately he gathered all the mice into his hands.

Daddy came up the stairs with a trap set with cheese. "Just drop the nest into the stove, Joe," he said.

"Into the stove! Oh, no!" Marly cried.

Joe was already at the top of the stairs. She clutched his arm, and when he turned and looked at her, he saw that she was crying. Tears were running in a real stream and dropping off her chin already, like a sudden rain. "It's people that spoil everything nice in the whole world!" she cried. "Think how happy those mice were in this house until we had to come! That's just the way my history teacher said people were—there were all those nice buffalos and everything. And bears. And deer and antelope and everything. And beaver. And then all those horrible old people came—"

"Marly, that's altogether different," Joe said.

Daddy stood listening in the bedroom door.

"It's not. It's just the same. Just because mice are little and helpless—"

"And useless. And they steal. They give people germs. They're nothing at all like buffalo." He gave her an absolutely disgusted look. "Oh, *girls!*" he said, and turned and disappeared down the stairs.

Marly stood still. She put her hands over her ears. The tears kept coming. She didn't hear the stove lid lifted up, but she heard it bang down again. Then the drawer in the bedroom closed, and Daddy came into the hall. "Now, Marly, it's not that serious," he said, and patted her as he passed. She didn't move, and when he got downstairs she heard him say to Mother, "Sometimes it makes you wonder, doesn't it? That funny child!"

After a while Mother called. Her voice was very firm. "Now, Marly, you get down here and help and no more of that silliness!" she said. So Marly helped again. When she helped make the beds, she didn't look at that drawer once. It was during supper that she heard the trap go off. Bang! She almost jumped out of her skin, even though she'd been listening for it.

"There it goes," Joe said. "That'll take care of the mother."

Marly tried not to think about it. What good would it

do now? And it wasn't hard to get happy again because right after supper who should come but Mr. Chris's hired man, Fritz, to take them to the sugar camp.

Fritz was a name Marly always thought of as plump and jolly. But this Fritz was lean and shy instead. He had come in a truck, and Joe and Marly got to sit in the back. Only Joe wouldn't sit, but stood bracing himself, so she did too. The white night-world looked wonderful and mysterious on either side of the road. They passed two houses, their windows lighted and shining out over the snowy hills. Our house looks like that, too, Marly thought, and knew why Mother had said to leave a light burning.

But if the houses looked prettier at night, why, goodness— the sugarhouse was the prettiest place in the whole world. "It's right over this hill," Marly said to Joe in the important voice of somebody who knows. "The minute you were out of sight this morning, why I just happened to see the smoke coming up, see—" She stopped. Now it was not smoke but the red glow of fire they could see. The door of the house stood wide open, and Mr. Chris was putting wood on the fire. He had opened two big doors and was shoving in huge chunks of wood as the truck came over the hill. Joe was off the truck before it even stopped. "Boy, oh boy!" he said, and ran.

The sugarhouse was a warm, beautiful red island in the middle of a cold white-and-black world. When Mr. Chris closed the firebox doors, there was a bright glow around the edges and the light of a lantern hanging from the rafters. The roof was high and glittering with steam. And in long pans, on a huge stove the whole length of the sugar-house, sap was boiling high. Bubbles like amber jewels tumbled up and up and *up*, breaking and rising and breaking. The wonderful smell seemed to rise with them and fly out to fill the night.

Mr. Chris's smile looked big and round in the lamplight, like a picture of Santa Claus. He was strong and huge and kind. He put his arm around Marly and gave her a hard squeeze.

"Come on in, everybody," he said. "Come in, come in!"

4 THE FIRST MIRACLE

"Some years now," Mr. Chris said, "are real good for sap. And some are not. This year the run started on the nineteenth of February. That's early. There was a big first run. What it takes is cold nights—freezing nights— and warmer days. Nobody knows why that combination brings the sap up, but it does."

Mother and Daddy and Mr. and Mrs. Chris sat around the end of the stove, just lounging around like people by a picnic fire. Mr. Chris told Marly the stove wasn't called by that name, but was an "evaporator" because it boiled the water out of the sap and left syrup behind.

"You can pump oil out of the ground, and water, too. But sap—you can't pump sap. It either decides to come up or it doesn't."

Marly stood by the side of the huge pans. You could look forever and forever into the bubbling, deeper and deeper, but your looking was always coming up again. She tried watching one bubble, all by itself, but she couldn't. It was gone, and another one was in its place too quickly. It was like ten thousand pots of taffy boiling all at once. The sap in the pans at the back looked like water, just as it did in the buckets on the trees, but each pan nearer the front was more and more golden, because each one was closer to being real syrup. Mr. Chris said he had to boil away *forty* gallons of sap to make *one* little gallon of syrup.

"How many gallons will one tree give?" Daddy asked, and Marly knew why he wanted to know. On Maple Hill there were about fifty maple trees. She could practically see Daddy's arithmetic getting ready to start working.

"An average tree will give twenty gallons in a season," Mr. Chris said. "That's usually a half gallon of syrup. Some seasons sap seems to be sweeter to start with, and it won't take so much. But there are trees—" Mr. Chris leaned forward as if he were telling a wonderful secret. "I've got one old tree, up by the pasture fence, that we hang six buckets on. That tree is five feet through, and I've known it to give us over two hundred and forty gallons of sap in one season." He looked proud about what that old tree could do, Marly thought. "I figure it must be over two hundred years old now," he said, and laughed. "But for a maple tree, that's young yet. Plenty of sap left for another hundred years."

Mrs. Chris laughed. "That tree is Chris's pet," she said. "I declare he goes out and pinches off its worms."

Mr. Chris opened the stove doors again and began shoving in more logs.

"Here, let me help with that," Daddy said. He picked up a good-sized one and shoved it in.

"When that tree dies," Mr. Chris said, still thinking of his pet, "it'll provide logs for another whole season of sugaring. Now that's being of some use in the world, isn't it? If a man could be as useful as that!" He kicked the doors shut again with his big boot.

Suddenly, as the heat rose from the logs, the sap in the

pans began rising faster. Bubbles rose like magic, faster and faster, and Marly stood back with a cry. "It's going to boil over!" she cried.

Every single pan was suddenly high, great waves rolling at the edges.

Chris laughed and reached over his head where a bucket swung from the rafters by a rope. "Now I'll show you a magic trick," he said.

In the bucket was a little bottle full of something white. It had a stick in it. Mr. Chris took the stick from the bottle and waved it over the pans, and—Marly stared and Joe gave a surprised whoop. Really like magic, the bubbles fell away as the stick passed over.

"Why, it is magic!" Marly cried.

Daddy laughed. "Cream, Chris?" he asked.

"I know," Joe said. "I read about that in science. It's the fat breaking the surface tension."

Mr. Chris said, "Kids are too smart nowadays. They don't believe in magic any more. Except Marly." Everybody smiled, and he reached out and gave her a little hug. She still stood looking at the fallen bubbles and then at the bottle and the stick in Mr. Chris's hands.

"Well, even if it's like Joe said, it's magic all the same, isn't it?" she asked.

They all laughed then, and Joe said, "Do you know what she said today? That a mouse was as important as a buffalo!"

"She did?" Mr. Chris glanced at Marly as he put the cream back into the bucket. "I don't know but what she was right if she was speaking of what's the biggest bother. See this bucket, Marly? I have to keep it hanging on that rope for the cream to be set in. If I don't, every time I turn my back the mice in this place drain the bottle dry."

"I'm surprised you don't let them have it," Mrs. Chris said. "I come out and find him *playing* with those mice. And do you know what he said when squirrels ate all the walnuts from our tree? *'Let 'em have those nuts, and I'll buy 'em another sack for Christmas.'* He's the same with those mice. They'd not think that cream was for them if he'd never given them any."

"Well," Mr. Chris said while everybody laughed, "the sugarhouse is a good place for mice to live in the wintertime. They've got to live, haven't they? Same as we do."

Marly was gazing up into Mr. Chris's face. "You never set traps for mice, do you?" she asked. "Or put their little babies in the fire?"

"Now, Marly—" Mother said.

But Marly paid no attention. "You wouldn't, would you?" she asked Mr. Chris.

"Why, no," Mr. Chris said. "They're right friendly little things. There's a deer mouse that comes every day, cute as a button with white feet and huge ears—looks like a donkey, with those ears. He and I are great friends. When I'm here alone hours and hours, lots of things happen." He winked at Marly and glanced at Mrs. Chris. "My wife doesn't know all about my funny friends," he said.

"Have you ever seen a mouse with a *thousand* babies?" Marly asked.

Mr. Chris looked amazed and shook his head. Joe said quickly, his face going pinker and pinker, "That was a meadow mouse, Marly. I read in a book—"

"There were mice all over that place. We've got to get rid of some," Mother said. "But for Marly—every spider, every creature has to live."

There was a little silence. Then Mr. Chris said soberly, "Well, feeling like that won't ever do her any harm."

"Except she'll have to cry more than she needs to." Daddy spoke suddenly, and reached out and took Marly onto his knee. Marly looked at him in surprise—and so did Mother, and so did Joe.

"Well, it's time to test this batch," Mr. Chris said, and took a wooden paddle from a hook on the wall. "Then everybody here gets a taste. Except Marly. She gets *two* tastes for being good to mice." He dipped the paddle into the last pan, and let the syrup run slowly off again.

"Does it spin a web when it's done, like candy?" Mother asked.

"Not quite. It sheets off—like that—" The last syrup hung over the edge of the paddle, and a great double drop came slowly down. "Some folks use a thermometer," Mr. Chris said, "but I like being able to *tell*. If you start using machinery for everything, you get so you don't just *know* any more, it seems to me. I've been doing this for forty years, ever since I had to boil in a kettle on a stone fireplace I built out yonder there, in the trees. I figure I should be able to tell without any help, now. Like the trees know when it's time to send up the sap! Now look at that—perfect, eleven pounds to the gallon or I'm a mighty poor judge."

He turned a little spigot at the side of the pan, and the syrup began to run out into a big five-gallon can. It was a golden stream in the lamplight. Over the can a cloth had been tied for the syrup to strain through. "Here, Marly, dip some in this cup and set it out in the snow to cool," Mr. Chris said. "Here, Joe, here's some for you."

Marly carried her tin cup carefully, reverently, and set it in a bank of snow. The syrup was so hot that before she

got it set down, the handle hurt her fingers. Joe set his on another bank of snow, and they stood waiting.

"We can boil a little down in the house for a while and then pour it on snow and make sugar-wax," Mrs. Chris said, following them. "I used to think wax was the best treat in the world. Folks around here used to serve it at sugaring-off parties during the season."

She showed them how the hot syrup went suddenly sticky in the snow, and how they could take a stick and make an all-day-sucker by poking it in and twisting it around.

Then the taste . . . It was like the smell, but stronger, sweeter, firmer.

"Take some syrup home and have pancakes in the morning," Mr. Chris said. "Did you bring the makings, Lee?"

"Of course," Mother said. "And a can of syrup from a grocery store in Pittsburgh!"

"How *awful!*" Mrs. Chris said.

Everybody laughed. Marly put her finger into the cup, and it was cool enough. She sat on the pile of wood in front of the fire and sipped. The syrup was better than the wax, she thought. The taste came through her nose, too, in a funny way. "Do you like it?" Mr. Chris asked. "Before, you got the *smell* of spring, Marly. Now you've got the *taste*. The sap is the first miracle that happens every spring. After all winter, with everything shut up tight, all of a sudden the trees are alive again."

"That *is* a miracle," Marly said. "Even in the park, down home. Every year."

Joe looked a little embarrassed, the way he might if somebody started to recite a poem.

"The sap running gives me a feeling I can't describe," Mr. Chris said. "Like it's the blood of the earth moving."

Everybody sat still as if they might be in church and Mr. Chris was giving the sermon. But it was different from church, with Mother and Daddy and Chrissie sitting on an old beat-up couch Mr. Chris had in one corner, and Marly and Joe and Mr. Chris perched on the piled-up wood. Fritz sat on a turned-over bucket, his boots stuck out in front of him. The fire spit and the sap boiled, and the drowsy heat and wavery lantern light and steamy smell were wonderful. Little fine drops fell sometimes from the ceiling.

"I wish somebody would sing a song," Mrs. Chris said. "Used to be we'd sit around the sugar fire and sing and sing."

"Like in the summer at our picnics," Mother said.

"Didn't you tell me Dale sang? When you were first engaged, Lee, I remember you said how beautiful his voice was."

"Oh, she thought everything about me was beautiful then!" Daddy said, and laughed.

"Your voice *is* wonderful, Dale," Mother said, not laughing at all.

"Was, maybe," he said. And to Chrissie: "I'm afraid I don't sing any more."

"Why not?" Mr. Chris asked in his big boomy voice. "Nobody who can sing should ever give it up. Not many folks can sing. I always said if I could so much as carry a tune in a sap bucket, I'd never give folks any rest."

"One song, Dale? These are old friends," Mother said. Her voice asked him hard, not telling him he had to sing, but just asking in a nice way.

Marly held her breath. She could remember Daddy singing, but it was a long time ago—before he went away, when she went to bed at night.

"That old one about the fox, that ballad would be nice," Mother said. "The children used to love that."

"I don't think I can remember all the verses—"

"Maybe I can help you out then," Mother said. "And everybody can sing the last lines together, the ones about the town-o."

For a minute Daddy sat looking tight all over. Then he stood up and put his head back and looked up at the rolling steam. His voice was little at first, but it seemed to get bigger and bigger.

"Oh, the fox went out one winter's night,
And he prayed to the moon to give him light . . ."

It was a wonderful story-song, the kind Marly thought was best of all. The fox took the fat duck home to his wife and babies, and the farmer was too late to prevent it. Daddy's voice got nicer with every verse, and at the end of every one the sugarhouse was as full of singing as it was of steam. Mr. Chris was a little bit out of tune, but it didn't matter.

When the song ended, everybody clapped and clapped and Joe said, "Dad, you know another one about a fox. I remember you singing it. About some hunters who asked a boy where the fox went, and he wouldn't tell them—"

"And the fox was tired and—" Marly began.

"That one's too fast until I practice. I'll sing it when you come back," Daddy said. "I'll practice every night." He looked at Mother, and she smiled, and everything felt good in a way Marly had almost forgotten.

"Well, you sure can carry a tune," Fritz said, with admiration.

Mother jumped up and said it was getting late and Marly looked as if she was going to fall off her perch any minute.

So they all walked out to the truck together, Mother and Chrissie and Marly walking last and looking back at the shining door.

"This is so beautiful, Chrissie," Mother said. "How you must love the sugar season!"

Marly jumped when Chrissie answered, because the way she spoke didn't sound like Mrs. Chris at all. Her voice was low and tight, a lot like Daddy's when he was cross and tired. "Love it? *I hate it!*" Chrissie said. Marly could hardly believe her ears. "He works too hard, you should be able to see that, Lee. Two years ago he had a heart attack just before the end of the season. But nothing can stop him—nothing! Do you think he'll take care of himself while there's work to do?" Her voice actually trembled, but they came to the truck where the men were talking and laughing together, and she said no more.

Marly felt wide awake again.

"Marly," Mr. Chris said, boosting her onto the truck, "your father says when school's out, you're coming up for the whole summer. You and I'll do some looking around, what do you say? I'll introduce you to every mouse I know. And every bird. And trees and flowers. Why, you haven't seen anything around here yet!"

"That'll be wonderful," she said. So she could go with him, she thought, and it wouldn't matter whether Joe would take her or not.

"You know what I'll promise you?" Mr. Chris asked. "Every week end you come until school's out, I promise you *at least one new miracle.*"

"All right!" she cried. The engine of the truck began to roar. Good night! Good night! The wide fields blinked under a moon. The woods looked dark and scary on the edges. But then there was a light—and another light—

"That next light's ours!" Joe said.

As they went into the house, Daddy began to sing again, without either being asked or told. He just suddenly started to sing that old song that starts, "Be it ever so humble . . ."

"That's the miracle for this week," Marly thought. It was better than the sugarhouse or the magic trick. She thought about it as she fell asleep in the very old bed where Mother had slept when she was a little girl.

5 PANCAKES

Mr. Chris kept his promise. He more than kept it, because once spring started one miracle at a time was nothing.

Actually it was two weeks before Marly even got back to Maple Hill again. The first week Mother had a bad cold and couldn't make the long drive. Daddy telephoned from Chris's house, and everybody got to talk to everybody. Daddy said it had been so warm for two days that week he'd worked outside in the sun. But still Mother was too sniffly to go.

Marly cried, wondering which miracle she was going to miss. Besides there wasn't going to be very much more sugaring. But nothing could be done about Mother's nose, after all. "Marly, you make me feel worse than I do already," Mother said, blowing and blowing her red nose.

So Marly didn't say another word.

Then there was a big blizzard, and a foot of snow fell in one night. Nearly April! Everybody had been going around with their coats over their arms; people in the streets smiled at each other. The park looked like something bright would be happening any minute; the lilac trees were dried out in the sun, and bumps started swelling out on the brown boughs. But when the cold came back, all in one night, it seemed as if winter was starting over, and everybody was disgusted. People didn't smile at each other, or if they did, you wouldn't know it because their mouths were tucked under their scarves and their collars. Marly loved her new boots and scarves and gloves in the fall. But now they looked dingy and felt heavy when she put them on.

Daddy wrote a long letter. "You people in cities don't need to think about the weather. Down there it's just a matter of getting yourselves out of one door and into another. But it's different up here! What a storm! Chris says nothing's as important in the country as the weather; he's given me an almanac."

The snow went away fast this time, though. When they finally got on the way again, the drive was beautiful all the way. Snow still lay in places where there was shade all the time, but it wasn't anywhere else. Some winter wheat fields were already green.

There was some gravel on the hill where they had stopped before, and the car went right along. But Mother stopped part of the way up the hill and said Marly and Joe could run up to the sugarhouse and see if Mr. Chris was there. But he wasn't. The buckets had been taken down from the trees and lay upside down on the ground. The big pans were turned over, and the fire was out.

Joe felt as sad as Marly did, she could tell. It was sad to see a place all empty and cold that had been so bright and warm before.

"Next year we'll see it again," Marly said.

"Sure. Mr. Chris will tell us the minute the sap's up," Joe said.

But when they came sadly out of the sugarhouse, a wonderful thing happened. Just a few feet away, looking at them,

47

stood a deer. It stood absolutely still with its ears and its head up. On its face was the most surprised expression Marly ever saw.

"Look!" she cried.

The deer leaped and turned and went off through the trees. It made great leaps without half trying, like a dancer in a ballet. Its white tail went up and down, up and down.

"Why didn't you just shut up?" Joe demanded. "You scared it off. I saw it as soon as you did; why did you say for *me* to look?"

"It was so lovely," she said.

He went marching off ahead as if she should feel ashamed. "Next time I'll just nudge you, Joe," she said. "But I was so excited this time. I'll tell Mr. Chris I saw the first miracle all by myself."

Then, in a little while, there was Daddy. He heard the car coming and came running down the hill to meet them, laughing and waving his arms.

"Dale, your own cooking is good for you," Mother said.

"It's Chrissie's dinners," he said, "and the air." He looked glad to see them, like some of the people you see in railroad stations. He hadn't looked like that at all when he first came home again.

"Look there," he said, turning around at the door, "look out over that swamp, Lee. See the color? That misty red? Chris says that's spring."

Before dinner he took them out to see skunk cabbages.

You'd think something named a skunk cabbage would be ugly and stinky, and Daddy said they sort of *were*, but they were interesting too. "Ugly and—" He paused and laughed and said, "Well, you'll see. Ugly *and beautiful*."

48

They were growing out of the ground along a little stream that was flooding down the valley just over Maple Hill behind the house. They had tight, smooth horns thrusting up here and there where the snow had all disappeared. They were green with dark-red designs. "Chris says they're the first real spring, after the sap," Daddy said.

Chris says . . . Chris says . . . Marly saw Mother smile when he said it over and over. They all went around the house and the yard to see everything Daddy had done. No trace of dust remained—no mouse leavings. The steps were mended. Mother said, "Dale, what shining windows! We'll see the sunset tonight." Then she took out the nice red and white curtains she had brought.

Daddy not only had a fire in the kitchen but in the living room too. The stove in there was called a Franklin, after Benjamin Franklin, who invented it with the help of a mouse—which Marly told Joe right away. (Only Joe said that was just a story in a book and wasn't true in the least.) Anyhow, that stove was like a little fireplace with little carved doors on its front and a nice place on it where you could put your feet to dry. "Oh," Marly sighed, "this is the nicest, prettiest, most comfortable house in the whole world. Can we stay up late? Can we? *Real late?*"

After supper the Chrises came over. They all sat around. Mr. Chris said he'd "pulled the buckets" in the sugarbush the day before because the buds were coming out on all the trees. "When the sap gets buddy, it's too strong and dark to be good any more," he said. "Only thing it's good for then is to boil down and sell to factories to put in chewing tobacco. But it's not worth the trouble."

"This is just like old times when your grandma was here, Lee," Chrissie said. "It's wonderful having your young ones,

49

but I keep looking around for her. I wish we could have the young ones and the old ones too."

Mr. Chris shook his head and smiled. "Let the young ones have it now," he said. "If all us old folks stayed around, we'd soon fill the world up, like mice."

Marly looked at him, quick.

"Sssh, Chris, don't start the mice again," Mother said.

But it was for Marly he had said it. She knew what he had meant: There were important things, and then there were things not so important after all.

When Marly woke up the next morning, there was another miracle right outside her window. The sun was coming up, and it was clear and frosty out. And there were ten million little crystals shining on every single branch of every single tree, down to the littlest twig. The tree right next to her window was a wilderness of shining threads, as if every branch, every twig, was spun from ice. Among the threads hopped the cold little black figures of the birds.

Marly felt as if she could never in the world look at it long enough.

She heard the door downstairs open and close again. Was Daddy going out into all that icy cold? When he first came home, he was always having chills, she remembered, and had to stay in bed mornings with the hot pad at his feet. Now there he went, out into a world of solid ice! She could hear the tree at her window clicking its boughs together when she leaned close to look.

But it wasn't Daddy, after all. It was Joe. He was dressed in his heavy coat and boots and gloves and had his green ear muffs on. Marly tugged at the window, but it wouldn't budge. So she pounded on it and shouted, and Joe turned and looked up at her. From even that distance she could see the disgusted look on his face. His mouth made motions that looked like the words "shut up!" to her. And then he turned and hurried off up the hill, and she watched him disappear.

Well! Didn't he think he was smart, though, going out on a secret adventure before anybody was up? She felt so jealous for a minute that she felt it go clear to her toes, which were folded up from the cold floor. But who wanted to go out into all that ice, anyhow? The last time Joe disappeared over a hill, he hadn't been such a great hero as he thought he was. When she thought of that, she felt better. If she wanted, she could go too. Why not? She dressed with her teeth chattering.

As she slipped along the hall she heard Daddy sleeping. Brrr! Even the kitchen was cold. She opened the door, and a blast of cold air came in. Goodness, she thought, Joe is welcome to all outdoors this morning! Who wanted to go out?

Then she had an idea. She would surprise everybody. She would build a fine fire and get breakfast all ready. And when Mother and Daddy came down, they'd stand by the door and stare and say, "Well, would you look at who's up and around so early? We thought we smelled something good."

Plenty of paper and wood and coal. She lifted the first lid on the funny old stove and stuffed in some of each. She would boil water and make coffee and then—then she would just mix up a batch of pancakes!

It was exciting to build a fire. She had never built a fire all by herself in her whole life. She filled the stove with things to burn and then she struck a match. The paper caught right away and flared out brightly. How lovely fire was, she

51

thought, and remembered Mr. Chris putting logs on the sugarhouse fire. She put the lid back on and waited.

But something began to go wrong with that fire right away. Instead of just blazing and getting warm, the way it should, little curls of smoke began to come up around all of the stove lids. She opened the lid to look. The paper had stopped burning and was just sitting there smoking. She found another match and tried again, coughing.

But the same thing happened—only more smoke came out this time, simply pouring out around every lid. She opened one and stuffed in a lot more paper quickly, and lighted another match. Now the smoke was simply pouring out, not only out of the paper but out of the kindlings too.

Oh, dear! What in the world—? And there was Mother's voice. "Dale! Something's burning!"

Daddy's feet hit the floor. He was running along the hall and down the stairs, with Mother right behind.

"Marly! What on earth—" He pushed her aside with a hard big sweep of his arm that almost knocked her down. He opened the stove lid and out came the smoke in another huge cloud, simply billowing. And then he put the lid back and reached around to the side of the stove and pushed something—and suddenly the smoke stopped coming. It was as magical and sudden as Mr. Chris and the cream.

Marly stood still and felt her heart beating harder and harder. Daddy stood looking at the stove; then he turned and looked at Mother, and then he looked at her. He was going to be madder than she had ever seen him in her whole life, she knew it. And she had seen him angry enough, so angry he couldn't even speak but turned and left the room and the house and didn't come back for hours and hours.

"What were you trying to do?" he asked. "Burn the house down?"

"Oh, our nice clean curtains!" Mother said.

"I just wanted to get it warm—and get breakfast. I was going to make pancakes, for a surprise—" Marly said. "Honest, Daddy, I only—" Her voice, her face, her whole body seemed breathless with fear as she looked up at him and he stood, absolutely huge in his pajamas, looking down. Then he turned back to the stove and opened the lids again and pulled out some of the things she had stuffed in. His hands went jerk, jerk, and his face looked hard. She waited for him to turn around again and say what he was going to say. And he would be right to scold her this time. It was stupid and terrible, what she had done.

"What a scare!" he said. "You put in too much, Marly, in the first place. Look—that's plenty for a start. And I should have told you about that damper." He turned. He was smiling! "One of my first mornings up here I did exactly the same thing. Now, you see—when the damper's back—"

He explained all about that big old stove, while she moved close to see. Relief flooded over her, and she felt light, light, light. There was such a huge gladness in her that it actually made a lump in her throat.

"You go on back to bed, Lee, until the house warms up," Daddy said. "Marly and I are going to build a fire in the other room too. She started this breakfast-thing, and she's going to finish it." But it wasn't scolding, the way he said it. It was a kind of teasing instead; there's all the difference in the world.

"Heavens, I'm too weak to get back up the stairs," Mother said. Marly saw how relieved she was, not only because there was no fire but because Daddy didn't seem to mind much about the smoke. "I thought the whole house was on fire. You know what went through my mind, just like that? *We haven't got the phone in yet. Everything will burn to the ground.*" Her laugh was shaky. She turned and disappeared up the stairs.

Daddy stood rubbing his hands over the fire. "Tell you what," he said, "you and I'll mix up those pancakes and take a plateful right up to her, and she can eat in bed for once, like a lady."

Suddenly, for no reason on earth that Marly knew, she ran to him and threw her arms around him, hard, and began to cry.

"Whoa, there!" he said. "No damage done!"

But it wasn't because of the fire she was crying. It was as if something all wound up in a ball inside of her had let go at the sight of him just that minute. She felt it all go soft inside. Everything! Even the lump in her throat went soft and went down and disappeared entirely.

"Well, Polly, get the kettle on!" Daddy said.

So she did. And they made the most wonderful pancakes she ever tasted in all her life. When Joe came in, all cold and red-faced, she was turning some pancakes over in the skillet. Daddy didn't ask Joe where he had been but just said. "Come on in and have some pancakes, a la Marly, Joe, all decorated with first-run Chris!"

Every single pancake was perfect, round and brown. Carefully she filled Joe's plate, and it was fun to see his face—it was so surprised. "Did you make these?" he asked. "Gee!"

Now Marly understood why Mother looked so pleased when they liked the things she made. After Joe said "Gee," he didn't say another single word until he had eaten nine pancakes in a row.

6 JOURNEY FOR MEADOW BOOTS

Joe always said he was going to be an explorer. When other boys wanted to be policemen and streetcar conductors and cowboys, he still said he wanted to explore. The minute he got to a new place, he had his "exploring look," and there was no use asking where he was going or whether you could go along. Marly knew you couldn't go until he knew everything around. But then he would begin to say, "I know a good picnic place . . ." or "There's a place deep enough to swim . . ." or maybe just "Marly, I can beat you to the top of that hill!"

Even in the city Joe explored by himself. But soon he began to show things like the park and the Natural History Museum and the Zoo and bridges and steel mills as if he himself had made every one of them. Besides, he acted as if he had made them *especially for you*. It was a nice way for Joe to be after the exploring was over. Marly was always forgetting, when he acted smart about knowing everything about everything, that soon he would take her along. It made her feel cross that a girl couldn't explore by herself, too, but Mother and Daddy would never let her.

At first she really thought a girl could and tried it once or twice. But in Pittsburgh she felt terribly little and worried, especially after one day when she got off the streetcar in the wrong place. The policeman she asked was very nice. But Mother was upset. Joe never got off the streetcar in the wrong place, or if he did, he never told. Marly imagined that if Joe got off at the wrong place he would just start exploring, wherever he was, and pretend he'd meant to get off there all the time.

Marly couldn't pretend like Joe could, because she was always getting scared. She could hardly ask a policeman where she was without getting a lump in her throat. And of course there weren't any policemen to ask on Maple Hill.

Once or twice Marly asked Joe if she could go along, but she really didn't expect he was ready to let her go. When he had been to the end of every little road and to the top of every single hill, then he'd be ready to show her some of the little things along the way. The reason she "slowed him up" was that she always wanted to stop and look at everything.

Marly had expected Mr. Chris would go places more than he did. But he was awfully busy in the spring. And then he wasn't supposed to walk much but would drive in the car to a place he wanted her to see and then walk along slowly and look at everything there was. He whistled to birds, and they answered him and came and hopped along the bushes by the road. There was a cardinal bird that came all the time. "He and his mate stay around here all winter long," Mr. Chris said.

He knew names for most of the flowers and trees. "But they're not always the same names Joe gets out of his field books," he said. "I just know the common ordinary everyday names that folks call things around here."

Two Sundays before Easter, Mr. Chris came early in the

morning while Marly was eating breakfast. "Hurry up," he said. "There's a big affair going on up in the woods."

A big affair? It sounded like a circus or a carnival the way he said it. "What is it? Can't you tell me anything about it?" she asked.

"Well—" He laughed. "It's a kind of beauty contest. You see, every spring the flowers around here have to fight it out to see who's going to be the prettiest. I try to get the bees to decide, but they won't. They seem to want everybody to win."

So it was going to be flowers. On the way she guessed. More spring beauties? No? Hepatica then, still another color maybe besides white and pink and blue and lavender? No? Another kind of trillium?

But what it actually was, as it turned out, Mr. Chris had his very own name for. He called these flowers "Easter candles."

"Most folks—and even Joe's books—call them after their roots instead of their flowers," he said, "because most folks have never seen them the way I'm going to show them to you now. They bloom so fast, for such a little while, it's easy to miss them if you're not right sharp and know when to expect them."

He made her cover up her eyes at the top of the hill and led her along an old lumber road for a while by the hand. He wanted her to be right smack in the middle of them, he said, for her first sight.

And goodness! Such a sight! When he said, "All right, you can open your eyes now," she did it, quick. It was more than anybody could believe who hadn't seen it for herself. All over the ground around her were great green leaves, each with a cleft in the side. Up through each cleft came a long thin stem, and on top of each stem stood a pointed bud exactly like a candle flame. Some were opening. The sun fingered its way through tiny green new leaves, and as it moved over the ground, as its light spread, the pointed buds opened. And more. And more. The petals were shiny white, like the inside of a shell. There were hundreds and hundreds and hundreds of them, turned to the sun.

"Tomorrow they'll be gone," Mr. Chris said in a hushed voice. "Hardly anybody ever sees them open like this. A fellow named Harry who lives on the other end of the mountain told me about them first, after I'd lived here twenty years or so. They call it bloodroot." He leaned down and cut one out of the ground with his pocketknife. It had a scarlet root, as bright as blood, so that was where it got its name. Some plants got their names from leaves, some from flowers, some from seeds, some from roots. And the oddest things were the ones like violets and roses, named from a color, so you had to call yellow and white and red ones violets and roses. "Used to be a notion that witches killed folks with the blood from this root," Mr. Chris said. "But of course it was just a tale. Anyhow, about witches. But it's absolutely true that if anybody eats it, his heart will stop in a day."

Marly stared at it, there in his hand, thinking about what Mrs. Chris had said about him and his heart. "Maybe you'd better not hold it in your hand, Mr. Chris," she said.

He laughed. "It's not that dangerous, Marly. This flower will keep a long time if you put it in water, so take it along with you and enjoy it. Show it to the folks. Picking blood-root flowers is no good unless you take the whole thing, root and all. Like spring beauties. They fade away in your hands."

59

If there were hundreds of bloodroot blossoms, there must have been thousands of hepaticas. They grew in huge masses of pink and white and every shade of blue, fairly tumbling down the hills. Folks thought, Mr. Chris said, that hepatica leaves were good for liver medicine because the leaves were the shape of livers. "So it's even called 'liverwort,' sometimes," he said, "that pretty flower! But it's got more names than you can shake a stick at. Some say it's a 'herb-trinity' because of the three leaves. Some call it a 'squirrel cup.' And some call it a 'mouse-ear.' Take your choice."

The very first trillium to bloom was deep red, which was likely why folks called it a "wake-robin." Then the white ones were everywhere, covering the floor of the woods thicker than the bloodroot flowers. Some were huge, at least six inches wide altogether. Mr. Chris knew where they grew the biggest. And he knew where to go to find little tiny ones, no bigger than appleblossoms, that were painted pink in their middles.

Mother smiled when Marly marveled at all the things Mr. Chris knew. "That's how Grandma was," she said. "She wrote down in her journal every day what had come up in the garden and what was in bloom in the woods and the fields, so finally she could look back in her journal and tell when any flower had bloomed any year. Then she could be watching for each one to come again."

"But Mr. Chris says you have to really watch," Marly said. "Some years things are early, and some years things are late."

"That's true, of course. I remember Grandma saying you couldn't bring things out of the ground until they were ready."

"Of course you can *help*," Marly said seriously. "Today I went all around helping trilliums."

It was true, and she had to explain. The flowers had to push their stems up through layers and layers of old brown leaves, and sometimes one of the leaves was extra tough and wouldn't move off, so the poor flowers were stuck tight together and couldn't open. The minute Marly broke off the tight old leaves, the flowers opened right away. It was a lovely thing to do, though such flowers always looked rather wrinkled and hurt for a day or so. The jack-in-the-pulpit had the same kind of trouble. Rescuing those odd little jacks, so stiff and tall under the green or purple striped awnings of their pulpits, was more fun than a picnic, though Joe said he'd never in his life heard of doing anything so silly.

She did it because Mr. Chris made her feel as if every flower was a particular old friend. It was grand to see his face when he noticed something for the first time that year. He could tell things apart that looked exactly alike to Marly —at least for a while—like Dutchman's-breeches and squirrel corn, and solomon's-seal and twisted-stalk with their tiny bells, and violets! Goodness, suddenly everywhere there were violets so thick you could hardly walk without stepping on them. They were white and yellow and blue and purple and spotted and striped. Some were tiny, and some were huge. And one tall yellow flower was called a dogtooth violet but was different and was really an adder's-tongue.

Marly brought Mother a different bouquet every day they were at Maple Hill.

Sometimes when she walked near home on the first little ridge, she'd get a strange feeling about the world. There

61

were lots of little roads that kept turning in among the trees and brambles and flowers. They were called lumber roads because trucks and wagons had made them years before when the land was timbered. Now trees were growing up again, but there were tangled old limbs in piles and ancient stumps overgrown with lichens and moss and little green leaves and ferns. If she stopped in the middle of all the thousands of things growing in every direction, she got what she called the "push-feeling." Everything was pushing up into the sun, trying to grow taller and bigger. She had never thought about it before in all her life, but all the miracles every week made her think about it. At first the wet brown leaves had lain over everything, everywhere, and then suddenly the peepholes started showing, and then through the peepholes came leaves and stems.

When she told Mr. Chris about the "push-feeling," he looked very serious about it. "Everything has its own sap, I guess," he said. "It's got to rise, that's all. Nobody knows why. It's like the sun in the morning."

Marly's really scary adventure happened during Easter vacation. One day she was on the lumber road back of the house when she saw something new and different that even Mr. Chris hadn't mentioned. Bright yellow. A different flower. It was beyond the old pasture, near the woods. It made her laugh to think of maybe finding a flower Mr. Chris had never met. She walked toward it, along the rail fence that marked the edge of Grandma's land. Rail fences were good to keep, Mr. Chris said, because bushes and little trees and things grew in all the corners, on both sides, and made safe places for building nests—as safe as thornbushes. Squirrels could run along the fences, too. Marly saw them trotting along the tops as if they thought the fences were their own special little highways.

At the bottom of the hill she saw the yellow flowers over the fence. They looked like puddles of gold in among the cattail leaves. She climbed over the fence and tried to go straight out toward one bunch of flowers. But the ground was all oozy underfoot. She felt with her shoe for a firm grassy place. And another one. And another. Finally she could reach the flowers if she stretched, and began to gather some. They looked just like buttercups now she was close, only bigger, with the same bright shine on their petals. Suddenly she heard something and looked up. It sounded like buffalo running in a herd, just the way they ran in the movies, pounding all together . . . But here, for goodness' sakes, there weren't any buffalo.

Then she saw them coming. Not buffalo. Just cows, young white-faced cows in a great crowd. And they were coming straight for her!

She dropped the flowers and started to make for the fence, but her feet went in. There wasn't time to search for the dry grassy places now. She splashed. Her feet sank at every step. She heard herself cry out and could hear her own breathing. She felt one shoe come off, deep in the mud. And then she stood on a little island of grass, too scared to move another step.

The cows had come pounding up to the very edge of the little swamp. There they brought up suddenly, all together. The ones in back pushed up into the front row to stare at her. They stood looking and looking, the whole big bunch of them, with round, wide eyes.

She stared back at them. They didn't move, except some-times to toss their heads as if they were angry at her for

being in a place where she didn't belong. Did cows object to people who picked their flowers? she wondered. Come to think of it, she had heard of yellow flowers called *cowslips*; maybe this was their special flower.

"Git! Go away!" she cried and waved her arms at them.

They looked at each other in a kind of amazement and then back at her. But they didn't move away. They only moved a little closer.

"Git!" she cried, the way she had always done to nippy dogs who chased her on her bicycle. She took one careful

step toward the fence, and the whole long row of them began moving again. How in the world was she ever going to get back over that fence? It seemed a mile away, and those cows didn't seem to want her to get there. The ends of the row moved in a little, so she stood in the center of their wide half-circle. Their eyes were like footlights, and she was right in the very middle of the stage.

Another careful step, and they all moved again. One spoke to her in a low voice. "Moooooooooooo!"

She began to talk to herself, saying, "They're not mean little cows at all. They're just *curious.*"

But the reason she said it was because she really wasn't

sure. They could just close in, if they wanted to, and tramp her under. Nobody would ever know where she had disappeared. Great, long shivers began to go over her from her head to her heels. Oh, Joe! she thought. If only he were here now! Once Joe had been with her when a cow came running over a field, and he just stood still and faced her, as brave as could be. And she stopped and mooed at him. He said, "I'll keep her interested while you get away, Marly." And he did. When she was over the fence, she turned around to see what he'd do to escape himself, and he had walked right straight up to that cow and was rubbing her long nose!

She would as soon have touched a lion.

But these cows were lots littler than that other one. They weren't much more than calves, she knew. But there were so many of them, and whatever one did, all the rest hurried to do it, too. One shook its head, and so did all the others. One took a step, and every single one of them took a step.

She tried another hummock. It was firm under her foot. But every cow moved as she took that one step. She could practically feel them breathing. How huge and steady and unblinking were their eyes!

I'll never go anywhere without Joe again, she thought, or without Mother, or Daddy, or Mr. Chris.

Then the horrible thought came that maybe she would never go anywhere again at all, with or without anybody. All the rest of time she would just be stuck in this terrible swamp . . .

"Git! Go away!" she cried again, and shook both her arms at them.

"Mooooo!" one said, and lifted its nose as it spoke as if making a signal to somebody far off. It tossed its head.

66

Every cow in the circle tossed its head then and said "Mooooo!" It was terrible.

"Please let me get to the fence. Let me get to the fence," Marly whispered to herself, like a prayer, and looked carefully at every green spot between her and the beautiful rails where a squirrel was running, stopping to watch her a minute and then trotting on again. If she jumped quickly there —and there—and if she didn't slip and fall—then she would be at the fence.

She had to try. There was nothing else to do.

She took a deep breath and looked straight at the cows and spoke in a low voice as friendly (and shaky) as it could be. "My name is Marline," she said, "but everybody calls me Marly. Do you belong to Mr. Chris? I'll bet you're Mr. Chris's cows, aren't you? I heard him telling Mother how many nice calves he had." They looked very interested. Some of them glanced at each other, and one of them actually nodded. Then they all nodded, the whole row. She took a step.

The whole row moved again.

I've got to—*I've got to* . . . Help me get to that fence. And she turned quickly and made one big leap, and another, and splashed and sank and ran through the water and the cattails, and clung to the fence. And then she was up and over.

Instantly the whole bunch of cows were right by the fence, looking at her. But she was safe.

She sat down on the ground, shivering horribly. And the row of cows looked very pleased, really, and satisfied just to see what she meant to do next. Now she saw how funny they looked, young and curious and wide-eyed. They were exactly like a row of children looking over the fences at the zoo.

She smiled at them, knowing they couldn't get over that fence. She was rather surprised when they didn't smile back.

All the time she crossed the field, they stood watching her. She could tell how wonderful and interesting they thought she was, all muddy and barefoot, and now she really knew they hadn't meant to worry her. They were just full of pushing, too, and they would have been sorry if they had pushed her into that swamp and lost her in the mud. She could see now how it had been. They had heard somebody strange splashing around in their drinking place and had to find out who it was.

Now she could laugh.

When she told the family at supper, everybody laughed. But Mother said it was a shame to lose her shoes, even though they were old ones. When she told Mr. Chris the next day, he said he'd take her over and introduce her to those cows properly, which he did. With him there she didn't mind facing the whole circle of them, although she did hang onto Mr. Chris's big hand.

The odd thing was that Mr. Chris said her adventure had probably saved the lives of every single calf! He should have known enough to fence that swamp off before this, he said, with an electric wire. Once he had a herd go in and eat those very flowers she was after. They were called cowslips sometimes, and sometimes marsh marigold. If cows ate too many, their stomachs swelled, and sometimes they died before the doctor could come to help.

What wonderful names he knew for *that* flower! Some called them "capers" and some called them "meadow boots." And when he was a boy, his mother had called them "crazy bet."

"I'm going to call them 'meadow boots,'" Marly said. "That's what they need where they grow."

After the wire was up, she and Mother went back for a nice bouquet and some supper greens. The leaves made fine greens, Mr. Chris said, before the spinach was ready. The cows came thundering toward Marly and Mother just the way they had before, but 'way back they stopped like magic. It didn't take them long to learn where the electric fence was strung. They looked a little sad, she thought, not to be able to come close enough to see what she was doing.

7 FOXES

It was the very last Friday before the very last week of school. As they drove up the hill Mother always called "the great slippery" because of that first time they were stuck on it, Joe suddenly said something wonderful to Marly. "You know, there's the queerest place up this side of the sugarbush. Moss all over on great big bumps. I'll show it to you tomorrow, if you want."

She held her breath. Had he explored and explored until now he had started to want to show somebody?

"We called those bump-things hummocks," Mother said.

"Some are ant-towns," Joe said. "The little ones." He smiled at Marly. "I'll show you tomorrow."

She could tell he had something very special on his mind. "Shall I fix a lunch?" she asked. He liked it when she fixed a lunch if it didn't slow them up too much getting started. "I can get up real early and fix it."

"That'll be swell," he said.

So at last, she thought, the time had come. Now she could go anywhere and be as safe as could be. Even if there were cows, with Joe she wouldn't need to be one bit afraid. She was awake so early the next morning that the birds had hardly beat her to it. As she hurried with the sandwiches and cookies and fruit, she kept humming inside, like a cat.

Joe was surprised to find her all ready when he came down—and how pleased! There she was, waiting on the back step with two neat sacks beside her, one for herself and one for him, only his exactly twice as big.

Joe explained some things on the way up the road. Maple Mountain was strange, Mr. Chris said, because it had swamps and bogs right up in its highest places. The humpy-bumpy meadows on top were part of its queerness too. Joe and Marly went from one hump to the other, opened some to watch ants, and looked at the queer moss and starry little plants on others. Joe had his magnifying glass, and they gazed into the strangest worlds, with funny little bugs tumbling around in the moss like animals in a jungle.

They went on to a little valley, then, and followed a brook that made one huge curve after another, doubling itself over like a coiled rope.

Joe said the curves were "meanders," and he showed her rocks in the stream bed that were full of ancient shells. They'd been left there ages ago when the ocean was practically everywhere. There were scrapings on the big stones and perfectly round stones that Joe said were shaped by huge slides of ice that were in that very spot about a million years ago—or maybe a billion. Marly couldn't think what the difference might be with those numbers, only that one was lots bigger than the other.

She felt proud of all Joe knew. Maybe Mr. Chris knew about flowers and birds and things, but Joe was the one who knew about bugs and the queer plants that grew on stumps and fallen trees. They had nice names, too. For instance, there were funny things like little plugged-up funnels, some gray called pixie-cups and some bright red called British soldiers. And there were odd little shelves that looked like they'd been made for fairies to sit on. Only Joe said they were just wood rot. On old logs there were tall black things called dead-man's-fingers. And one funny toadstool was bright yellow, called a jack-o-lantern, that Joe said really gave light at night.

"Joe, you know more things than Mr. Chris," Marly said.

To her surprise he said, "Oh, no, I don't! Nobody knows more than Chris. Who do you think told me most of that stuff? We came out here last week, and Chris showed me some things I wanted to show you. In the fall around here there are mushrooms all over, if you know where to find 'em. One of Mr. Chris's hired men, before Fritz, used to gather quarts and quarts and sell 'em to an Italian in town and make a mint of money every fall."

She hardly heard the last of it. "Joe," she said, "Mr. Chris didn't climb clear up this hill, did he? Why, if Chrissie heard about that—"

Joe went red. He pretended not to hear what she was saying but leaned over and then knelt right down on the ground. "Look there, at that striped beetle. Blister beetle, that's who! When we get to a pool I found, I'll show you some diving beetles too. You ever see a whirligig?"

"Joe—did he?" she asked. "Because he shouldn't. Chrissie told me to look out for him and not let him climb even the littlest hill. And this one—" She looked behind them at the steep path.

"You know, the other day I saw a huge bumblebee

caught in a lady-slipper," Joe said. "Couldn't get out to save him. I could hear him a block off, roaring—"

Marly interrupted. It wasn't because she wasn't interested in that bumblebee, but Joe had to know about taking care of Mr. Chris if he didn't know it already. "Joe, you and Chris were supposed to go into town that day in the car."

He stood up suddenly and turned to her. "I guess you'll go right and tell!" he said. "Just like a girl, can't keep anything to herself! Sure we went to town. We talked with that man in the restaurant, see. He buys all his syrup from Mr. Chris and says it's the best syrup in the world. He buys all his apple juice from Mr. Chris, too. And he says he used to buy chestnuts—but that's been years and years. After, Mr. Chris and I came up here, and he showed me those old chestnut snags—see, along there? There used to be so many you could get a half bushel of chestnuts in an hour."

"Joe, Mr. Chris didn't walk clear up here, *did* he?" Marly asked. "You shouldn't *ever* let him, Chrissie said. She told me we've got to help, because when he gets interested in showing people things, he just forgets."

"Okay, okay. We walked real slow. And he told me how this country used to look. Lots more forest than now. Between diseases like the one that killed all the chestnuts, and then people timbering their land, he says almost all the virgin forest is gone now."

Marly stood still. As if what Joe said had started the sound, she suddenly began to hear the whine of a saw. From Mr. Chris's place? "Joe, Mr. Chris isn't cutting down trees, is he? Just for money? He told me he never would."

73

"Of course he's not." He looked disgusted that she should even ask. "But I want to watch them cutting that tree. It's an old maple," he said.

As they walked, the whining of the saw grew louder and louder until it seemed to make huge circles of sound through the woods. They made a big circle and came finally to the sugarbush.

Mr. Chris was there with Fritz and a strange man with an electric saw. The old tree at which the saw was working was dead except one great branch that stood green among the masses of brown boughs. It was over a yard thick and was giving the saw a very hard time of it.

Mr. Chris waved to Marly and Joe as they came. When he talked, he had to shout over the ugly whining of the saw. "A grand old tree," he said. "A good sugar tree, for years and years. I've tapped it every season until this last one, for at least thirty years. We used to boil the sap right over there—had a long oven and one big pan. You can even see the old stones where the oven was."

Joe and Marly stood watching. They didn't try to talk, and Mr. Chris didn't say any more, either, for a while. The saw's humming was almost a scream as it got near the center of the trunk. Mr. Chris leaned close to Marly's ear. "When she falls, we'll count the rings and see just how old she is," he said.

A red squirrel began scolding from another tree. Mr. Chris looked up and shook his fist, laughing. "It's all right, old fellow," he called. "We're leaving you your butternut tree. But this old maple is going to come home with us and keep us warm this winter."

The squirrel sat looking at him, its paws folded in front as if it might be saying its prayers. Then the great maple began to crack and groan, and the squirrel turned and vanished into a hole. Fritz shouted, "Watch out! She's coming down!"

Like a giant, the great tree fell. Its immense dead limbs struck the ground first and broke, crashing, and it sagged and roared and seemed to fight with the air. For a minute it lay trembling all over. Then it was still.

Marly wanted to cry. But Joe laughed and yelled, "Hurrah! Boy, oh boy!" and before the tree had really settled down, he was into the branches. And then he was counting the rings. That tree had been growing for over a hundred years.

It was dusk as they started for home. Now that the saw had ceased to whine, the silence seemed immense and wonderful. They could hear the rustling of the trees that still stood up straight into the air.

Suddenly, just as they came to the hummocky place, Joe clutched Marly's arm. And then, without warning, he laid his hand hard across her mouth, whispering, "Ssssh!"

It was lucky he saw it first or she might have yelled the way she did when she saw the deer. Joe whispered, "Look!"

Up on one of those bumpy hummocks, just standing with its huge bushy tail straight out behind, was a red fox. It stood looking down the hill, one paw lifted like a puppy paying attention to everything. Then it leaped suddenly to another hummock and stood there, looking. The sun was down, and a weird light was over everything, so the fox seemed to have a shine all over.

Marly and Joe didn't move. Neither did the fox. Finally, then, without a sound, looking like a colored shadow, the fox slipped from the hummock and was gone. It disappeared into the ravine, by the brook.

"I'll bet she's got a den around here," Joe said. His voice was low, and when he walked, he walked easy in a certain way he knew, the way he had learned Indians walked. Marly couldn't hear him past ten yards. She wanted to call, "Don't go out of sight, Joe," because dark was starting and there was that strange light, rather eerie, as night fell over Maple Mountain. But she didn't call. She didn't make a sound.

In a minute she was glad she hadn't. Joe came slipping back out of the shadows, beckoning.

"Ssssh! And don't fall over anything!" he said.

"Joe, what is it?"

"Sssssh . . ."

At one place the hill went suddenly down, rocky and steep. At the top Joe took hold of her arm hard, and then he pointed with his other hand.

In the dusk were five little foxes, playing together. They tumbled about like puppies. They chased each other. They made little growly sounds, pretending to fight. They were all red, except for their black pointed noses and their sharp black ears, and each one had a white tip on its long red tail.

Joe and Marly watched until they couldn't see a thing but the white tips on the tails. Then these too vanished.

Joe led Marly toward home, over the hummocks, holding her by the hand. She had never loved him so much in all her life. "Joe, if it hadn't been for you, I'd never have seen anything like that. Not *ever*," she said.

"Why not? I see things all the time," he said. But she could tell he was pleased that she had said it.

The Chrises and Fritz were at the house when they got back. As soon as Marly got into the door and saw them, she cried, "Guess what we saw, Joe and me, up by the high pasture. Some *fox* . . ." And then she said, suddenly, "Ouch!" because Joe had given her a good big pinch.

He hadn't done it soon enough. She already had the word out of her mouth.

Fritz leaned forward in his chair. "Foxes, huh? So that's where they are!" He turned to Mr. Chris. "I knew they were around close somewhere, didn't I, Chris? I can go in the morning. Maybe if I go before light, I can grab the whole bunch."

Grab them? Marly felt her eyes go wide. "Fritz, you don't mean you want to catch those little foxes, do you?" she said. "Why, this one has five babies, the cutest little puppies—"

She saw Joe's look. Oh, she never never knew when to keep her mouth shut! That's what his look said to her, as plain as day.

"Five little ones, huh? No wonder she's been busy," Mr. Chris said. "How many chickens does that take every day? Every day for a solid week that she-devil has been at my chickens. We put the flock in the coop last night, and she got in under the wall. Or her mate it was. If they aren't the cleverest—"

"And that dog, Tony, doesn't even notice any more," Chrissie said. "I tell Chris he's too old for a watchdog now. He sleeps like a stone."

Marly's mouth felt dry. "What are you going to do?" she asked. She didn't dare even look at Joe.

A little silence fell. Everybody suddenly remembered Marly and those mice.

"Well," Mr. Chris said, and gave a queer little cough, "to tell you the truth, Marly, this country is overrun with foxes the past few years." He turned back to Fritz and Daddy as if he'd rather not talk to her about it any more. "There's a good big bounty on them now, and if you want to fix the pelts up, you can get more." Then he looked straight at Joe. "You show Fritz the place in the morning, Joe. Maybe you can get a shot or so yourself."

Was this Mr. Chris? Marly gazed at him.

"Tell you what, we'll split the bounty, Joe, no matter who gets 'em," Fritz said. He was a good shot, Marly knew; she'd heard them tell about how many rabbits and pheasants and squirrels Fritz got in hunting season.

"Okay," Joe said.

Marly turned to him in unbelief. After seeing those little foxes playing as the sun went down! "Joe, you wouldn't!" she said.

"Those things eat mice, too," Mr. Chris said hastily. "Marly, they eat hundreds and hundreds of mice. If I just had livestock and grain or even orchards, I'd say the more foxes the better. But chickens—"

Marly couldn't manage another word or stand to hear one. Everybody was agreeing, and she knew there wasn't any use. If even *Joe*—after what he had seen! Suddenly

79

the words of the song Daddy sang sometimes came back to her. Not the song about the fox coming for the big black duck, heavens no! But the one about the cruel hunters in their red coats and the nice boy who felt sorry for the fox and refused to tell them which way it had gone. Had Joe forgotten?

When the Chrises and Fritz went away, Fritz called back to Joe that he'd be calling by real early, maybe about five o'clock. Joe went right up to bed, then, without a word, and Marly felt herself go cold all over. She reached for Daddy's arm as he started for the stairs. "Daddy— about the foxes—"

"Marly, please," Mother said. "There's no earthly use of your worrying about things like that. You've got to learn."

"I was only going to ask Daddy to sing tonight," Marly said. "Those foxes made me think about the fox songs."

Daddy and Mother looked at each other.

"First the one about the fox stealing the goose," Marly said to get them off the track of what she meant to do. Then, she thought, if Daddy would sing the one about the hunters and the wonderful kind boy who wouldn't tell where the fox went, Joe would understand what she was going to say when she went upstairs. He couldn't help but understand, after that song.

"Well, all right. Just those two, then," Daddy said. "You know, Lee, I'm getting so I can do the hunting song pretty well again."

And he really could. The first verse about the hunters coming and the horns blowing and the scarlet coats went really fast. Marly opened the door to the stairs so Joe would be sure to hear.

" 'Say there, youngster,' the huntsmen cry,
    'Say, have you seen the fox go by?
    Galloping, galloping, galloping, galloping,
    Galloping, galloping over the hill?' "

"Now," Marly thought, and opened the door a little wider. This was the verse for Joe to hear.

"But would I be telling them? No, not I!
    That I saw the fox go wearily by?
    Wearily panting, worn and spent,
    Would I be telling the way he went,
    Galloping . . . galloping . . . galloping . . ."

Daddy was wonderful, the way he made the words sound slow and tired as if the poor fox was ready to drop. Then suddenly he shouted the last two words: "No! Not I!"

It made Marly's hair wiggle every time she heard it, it was so wonderful. But especially tonight. She kissed Daddy good night more fervently than ever before and went upstairs, closing the door after her. But Joe's door was closed, and his light was out.

So he didn't want to talk about it.

But she did. She had to. She opened his door just a crack and whispered, "Joe . . ."

No sound.

"Joe," she said.

Suddenly he spoke. He wasn't in bed at all. He was sitting in the dark by the window. "Just shut up for a while," he said in a low voice. "Can you? I've got to figure out what we can do. If I went over and threw rocks and tramped all over there where the den is . . . See, if I could just scare them out of there before Fritz can get there . . ."

81

"Oh, Joe, of course you can!" she said. And then, excitedly, "Tonight? Joe, way over to the hill tonight?"

His voice sounded disgusted. "I can't very well wait until morning this time, can I? If Fritz ever heard of me doing a thing like that, he'd think I was crazy. Why, there are seven of 'em right there. Four dollars' bounty apiece! That s a lot of money!" She felt his eyes through the dark. "If you just didn't have to tell everything you know! Sometimes I think it's better never to tell you anything—or show you anything."

"Joe, I'm so sorry. Honest, I'll never, never tell anything again. Why, I just thought Mr. Chris and Chrissie and Fritz would love those little foxes." She looked beyond Joe, out of the window. It was deep-dark and scary, and she shivered. "Joe, it'll be horrible to go clear over there past all those bumpy places and everything in the dark."

"If I took a light and then just shot at the ground near the den," he said, thinking aloud, his voice very low. "I guess you could go along and hold the light, couldn't you? Just so we get 'em out of there."

"Joe—you mean I can go?" She felt a glow everywhere, a happiness that was like suddenly running out of the cold into a warm, bright house. She had put the foxes in danger, but now she could go out into the night and help make them safe again.

"The trouble is maybe they'll fight. I don't know. Look what it says in my *Field Book*." She closed the door, and he turned his light on and showed her the place. "Look— 'Male feeds female and young, and leads enemies away from den at risk of his life.'"

"We're not enemies," she said. "It's Fritz he should lead away."

"Too bad Father Fox doesn't know that, now isn't it?" Joe asked. "You say the silliest things I ever heard. But it's not a question of leading Fritz away—he knows where the den is now."

"If only I hadn't mentioned it!" she cried.

"Well, that's spilled milk now. You didn't know." He sat staring at the book as if it might give him an idea. "Maybe if we built a little fire by one door we could smoke 'em out the other, like bees," he said. "They always have a front door and a back door."

She was enchanted. "Joe, how clever—a front door and a back door—"

"Now just act like you're going to bed," he told her. "But put on some warm socks and things. We'll go as soon as Dad and Mother are asleep."

What ages it seemed before Daddy and Mother came upstairs, before they were finally finished in the bathroom and had climbed into bed, before Daddy finally began to snore! Marly heard Joe's door open. She was so excited she could hardly breathe, and a funny little pain started at the back of her neck. Moving as silently as possible, she followed Joe's shadow down the stairs. He was getting the flashlights out of the drawer. Then he got a pocketful of matches and a rag and the can of kerosene.

Goodness, but that road was dark! Joe led the way, only flashing a light once in a while and then very briefly. They passed Chris's house, all dark, and went on to the field and the pasture. How wide and high the night was! Marly had never seen it look so huge. She looked up with the biggest, highest feeling she'd ever had in all her life as they started up the hill. If it hadn't been for Joe walking close ahead, she knew she'd have been scared enough to die in her tracks. Shadows hung over the road and slipped around the trees and stones when Joe flashed the light.

At the top of the slope where the den was, Joe stood still and waited for a long time. Was he afraid? Marly was scared to think he might be, because if *Joe* was scared . . . Well, that meant it was really dangerous. But he wasn't scared. He was only planning what to do. After a while he spoke quite loud, and she jumped. She had expected he would whisper. "Look, Marly, you shine both flashlights into the hole, see, when I find it. I'll fix this rag, and then we'll light it and stuff it in and run. See?"

"Where'll we run?"

"Back up here. Then we can watch and see what they do."

That was exactly what they did. Joe made a big noise going down the slope; he let rocks roll under him and everything. The sooner the foxes were scared now, the better, of course. They had come to scare foxes.

"Here's the den," he said. It was a real big hole, with grass over the top like a huge eyebrow so nobody would ever have seen it from above. Marly's hands shook so her lights went wobble-wobble. The rag flared at once, the minute Joe struck the first match, and Joe tossed it in.

And then they ran, stumbling and slipping as they climbed.

They didn't have long to wait. Out of the other door came a long slim shape, and another, and another smaller, and then a whole quick row of them. The flame showed them as plain as plain, and besides Joe suddenly turned a flashlight full onto them. There was a flashing of eyes. And that was all. The rag died down and went out, and there wasn't a sound.

They waited. Far off, a dog barked. Or was it a dog? "I'm not sure the father was here, even," Joe said. "I only saw one big one. Maybe he'd gone off to hunt, and she's calling him."

Once more they heard the barking. It sounded far off. "If that's her barking, she's gone a long way already," Joe said. "I don't think they'll come back here. But in case they do, we'd better put some rocks and things in the doors. Are you too tired?"

"No, I'm not tired at all." It was true. She was too excited to be tired. She worked right beside him, and they put lots of rocks in both the doors.

"Well, I guess that's all we can do," Joe said.

Now that it was over, Marly was so tired she could hardly walk, but she didn't say so. When they got home, they didn't make a sound. Except right at her door Joe suddenly took her arm and squeezed it hard and whispered, "Now keep your mouth shut about this, see? Not a word!"

"Not a word," she said.

"Honest?"

"Honest, Joe. Cross my heart."

That was the last she knew until she heard Fritz give a little honk at dawn. He went everywhere in the truck because he had so much to do from one end of the farm to the other. Joe went down the stairs, and Marly watched from the window. Joe had his gun. She lay shivering so hard she thought she'd be better up. So she went downstairs and built a fire that really burned. She even mixed biscuits.

"Well, look who's up already!" Daddy said. He went outside to listen, and came back and asked, "Have you heard any shots yet, Marly?"

"No," she said.

"And I know you were listening." He patted her hand. He thought he understood, she thought, but this time he was all wrong. He didn't know *half*. And she would never tell, either, in this world or another.

They didn't ever hear any shooting. Not that morning! Soon they heard the truck instead. Joe got out at the gate and waved his gun to say good-by as Fritz drove away. Marly's heart was beating fast when Joe appeared at the door. She gave him one look—and he winked.

"Funniest thing," he said. "We went right to that place, and there wasn't a sign of a fox. Den's all full of stuff. Fritz said he never saw anything like it before."

Marly ran to look at the biscuits. They were done, huge and brown. She felt as if she would burst clear out of her skin with joy, so she began to sing. "Galloping . . . galloping . . . galloping . . ." Her voice cracked when she sang "No, not I!" because it was on a note too high for her. But she didn't care.

"I wonder—" Daddy said.

But he didn't say what he wondered, and nobody answered.

8 HARRY THE HERMIT

"Goodness, but I'd hate to live in two places at once all the year around," Mother said. "I'm tired of packing all this stuff back and forth." But she was looking happy whether she was tired or not. They would not have to come back to the apartment all summer long.

The drive was in daylight this time, all the way, even though it had taken them a long while to get everything ready and the apartment locked up. Clear from the bottom of the hill they could see Daddy come out and wave.

Well, he's got an apron on," Mother said. "He must be getting our supper."

And he was. Not only their supper but Mr. Chris's and Fritz's and Chrissie's besides. He was so busy he forgot to ask whether their report cards had been good or even whether they had been promoted. Of course he was pleased when they told him, and said, "I knew there was plenty of reason for a good big celebration around this place!"

When the Chrises came, he was looking hot and red as he leaned over the oven. "The one thing I dare fix for a good cook like Chrissie is broiled steak," he said, "so that's all we're having."

"*All?* As if there was anything in this world any better!"
Chrissie said.

The whole evening was wonderful and jolly and special.
It was the best night they had ever had at Maple Hill,
except of course that first night at the sugar camp. When
all the steaks were gone, they sat and sang and talked and
told stories. Then the Chrises and Fritz said they had to
go home *sometime*, and shook hands with everybody all
around. At the door Mr. Chris said, "Now you folks don't
have to leave us again until the leaves turn."

"Long before *that*, I'm afraid," Mother said. "I remember
how Grandma used to say we left before the prettiest sights
of the year."

Marly stood on the porch, breathing the flowery smells
and looking at the bright stars. "Autumn can't be prettier
than this," she said. "It just *can't*."

The moon seemed to nod at her through the leaves of
the vines that hung from the eaves around the porch.
Those leaves were all sizes now, from tiny new ones to big
spreading full-grown ones. Mr. Chris seemed to be thinking
about them, too, for he said, "The Virginia creepers seem
to like the whole family at home at once, like us. Little ones
and big ones, all together."

The next morning Marly lay a long time, just listening.
So many different birds singing! Leaves were rustling outside her window; now that it stood open she could hear
the littlest sound. She could even hear water splashing down
the hill, as restful to listen to as the pattering of rain.

Now we are really at Maple Hill. *Really*, she thought.
She got up and dressed and ran downstairs and straight
outdoors into the bright sun. Dew shone everywhere, but
it was warm. If you weren't as hungry as all three bears

put together, she thought, you wouldn't have to build a fire all day long.

Somebody shouted "Yoo-hoo!" from the top of the hill. Of course it was Joe. He couldn't stand not to let her know he was up earlier than she was, no matter *how* early she might get up. But she waved and called "Yoo-hoo!" right back at him.

Then she forgot about Joe, because she found something lovely right along the side of the house. A long row of little red points was sticking up out of the ground, with curly folded-up leaves. Rhubarb. She had never seen rhubarb outside of a market in all her life. She was stooping over it when Daddy came out of the house. "I found that old row of rhubarb," he said proudly, "and it's coming along fine. And do you know, Marly, there's asparagus coming, too."

Then he told her of all the things that were in his garden. He took her proudly along every row and showed her the little crookedy rows of tiny leaves. He knew what all of them were, even though they looked very much alike, except the carrot-feathers.

That day was the beginning. It was the same from then on—one wonderful surprise after the other. Early spring was not a bit more amazing than early summer, because the big pushing went on and on. Things weren't coming up any more, but they were getting bigger and bigger and *bigger*, every day. You could practically measure the growing, especially—as Joe complained—when you had to mow the grass, and especially—as Daddy said—when you had to keep after the weeds in a garden.

Ferns, which had been nothing but tight hairy little curls, stood huge along the roads. In Mother's flower garden she kept finding things that Grandma had loved. Buds and then yellow roses appeared on the bushes by the porch. Weeks before, there had been daffodils springing up among the old weeds, and fragrant hyacinths, and blue flags. English violets appeared when the beds were cleaned out. Under the trees and on the shady side of the house were lilies of the valley, in clumps so thick one could gather whole brides' bouquets, as Mother said, and never notice where they had been picked.

Then lilacs, white and purple, sent waves of perfume over the porch in the evenings when a breeze sprang up.

Red raspberries appeared in the wilderness beyond where Fritz had plowed for Daddy's vegetable garden. Every morning early, every evening until it was too dark to see, Daddy worked in his garden or among the vines. When Mr. Chris came for a visit, he and Daddy stood outside or sat on the grass. They never seemed to run out of talk about seeds and weeds and bugs and sprays and fruit, as Mother and Chrissie seemed never to run out of talk about flowers and jelly and jam.

"I thought Marly asked a lot of questions," Mr. Chris said once. "But I think Dale here takes the prize. If Fritz and I don't hump ourselves, he'll be growing vegetables that'll take every ribbon at the Fair."

"We'll be gone before the Fair," Daddy said. He said it as if he'd surely get all the ribbons if he wasn't gone. And no wonder, the way things grew for him.

Fritz even seemed a bit jealous about Daddy's garden. "This place hasn't been planted for a long time," he said. "It's fresh and rich."

Once in a while Fritz came by and said Daddy had worked long enough—and then they went fishing. Of course

Joe went, too, and Mother and Marly had, as Mother said, "a fine female time." They didn't have to cook perfect pots of things every meal but ate up all the leftovers. Then, when the men came home, they ate fish, wonderful sizzling pans of crisp little fish. Fritz always got some whether Daddy did or not. And Joe—Fritz said Joe was a born fisherman.

"Maybe," Marly heard Daddy say to Mother one warm summer night as they sat over their plates of fine little bones, "it's still possible for a family to live entirely off the land."

"Entirely?" Mother asked, and shook her head. "What about *shoes?*"

Marly knew what Mother meant. Plenty of things didn't just grow. Every time there was talk about living off the land, somebody ended by saying, "How did those people manage, in the old days, going right out into the wilderness the way they did?"

One night Mr. Chris told them a story of two little boys who were the very first white people to spend a whole winter in this very valley. Their mother was a widow with lots of children and a cow. She brought her family and the cow to start a farm, arriving in the spring. When winter came, she went back to a far-off town where she lived, leaving two of her sons to keep the cow and the little house they had all built together.

"Those boys managed fine, I guess," Mr. Chris said. "The older one was only fourteen. The next spring the family came back again, and then they stayed. You can see that family name all over this country now, on dozens of mailboxes."

"I could do it easy," Joe said, "if I had a house and a cow."

"And of course a gun," Fritz said.

"There's an old fellow near here who lives about like that," Mr. Chris said. "We call him Harry the Hermit. Lives at the end of the mountain, south, just above that pond where the ducks landed."

"If you can call it *living*," Chrissie said, and held her nose. "He has goats. Folks say they live right in with him in the winter."

The next morning Marly was not a bit surprised to see Joe headed south.

"I wish I could see the hermit, too," she thought, enviously. And then she had an idea. Why not? She could just start out after Joe, keeping him in sight and not calling or anything. He hadn't asked her, but if she just came, what could he do?

She found she could go fast enough to keep him in sight, except just over the tops of the hills. He wasn't hurrying. Past Chris's place, he turned on a little road, and pretty soon, sure enough, there was a lovely pond. Joe walked around it, looking in and stooping down, and for a while she thought maybe he wasn't going on at all. But pretty soon he started out again. Then he stopped by a tipsy mailbox gazing up a hill. First there was a wide meadow without any trees, just waving grass. Beyond the meadow stood a little house. Behind that was a still littler barn, which looked queer in Pennsylvania where barns were usually ten times bigger than their houses. A steep, rocky path came straight down the hill, ending at the mailbox where Joe stood.

She saw Joe walk around the box. Looking for the name,

maybe. Then he looked at something in it. A letter? Surely he wouldn't look at anybody else's mail! There were laws and things to keep people from doing that. And in full sight of the house.

She decided to call him. It was time he knew she had come along.

He didn't seem in the least surprised to see her. When she came walking down the road he said, "Didn't you think I saw you? I knew you were following me all the time. But look here, Marly—what do you think of this?" There was a note standing in the box against a little pile of honeycombs. The note said, "Take honey. Leave money. Gone for the day." Lying beside the note was a quarter and a nickel.

"He sure trusts people, doesn't he?" Joe said, and gazed up toward the house. "If he's gone for the day, why don't we just look around?"

There was never in this world a more wonderful place for looking around. The house was of wooden planks, very plain, painted gray. The back door stood wide open, and flies buzzed gaily in and out of holes in the screen.

"Don't stand looking in, Joe," Marly said. "I don't think it's polite to look into people's houses when they're not home." But Joe went on standing there, looking and looking. Pretty soon he turned to her and said, "If you want to see something interesting, come look. Fritz told me this old man makes wooden chains. And there are dozens of 'em, all sizes, hanging all over the walls."

So she looked too. And when they turned away from the house, they saw another chain standing against a huge oak tree in the yard. It was only partly made, from "a log as long as Joe-and-a-half," as Mr. Chris would say it. The huge links were only partly cut out, so it looked rather like one of the totem poles in the museum, scallops going down four sides.

"You can tell how he makes them, from that one," Joe said, excited. "Fritz tried to tell me, but I couldn't see what he meant. The hermit showed him how. See—each scallop and its opposite scallop will make one link for the chain. When the wood's all cut out, the links are free—see how they'll be?—yet all fastened together."

She didn't see, really, but she didn't say so.

"Why, I'll bet I can make one of those," Joe said.

Then they explored down the hill. There were cunning steps cut into the slope all the way down and set with flat stones. Moss had grown over the edges, and they were all tucked in with grass. They led to a tiny stone house, invisible from every direction. Only its steep roof could be seen from above. It had a tight little door about four feet high.

Joe began to open it right away, and Marly said, "Joe— do you think you should?"

He gave her a look. "What do you think's in there— witches?" he asked. "He won't care. Fritz knows him. Besides he's away, and we won't touch a thing."

It was a springhouse, just the kind you read about pioneers having before there were such things as iceboxes or refrigerators. There was a dipper hanging on the wall, made from a gourd, and around a deep dark pool of water were set those same flat stones. The opening where water was dipped up was no bigger than one bucket on its side. All around the edges on clean damp stones were honeycombs and lovely neat, round light-yellow cheeses! There was a big flat pan of milk, too, with a cheesecloth stretched over the top and held down at the sides with stones.

It was like looking at long ago. Marly stooped down and dipped up a dipperful of water. It was clear and cold. Suddenly, just as she was going to drink it, they heard somebody coming down the steps.

"Joe!" Marly's hand trembled and the water spilled all down her front, over her shoes. "What if that's *him?* And here we—"

He gave her his strongest for-heaven's-sake-shut-up look. And she did. They stood absolutely still, and water went drip-drip, and the steps came nearer. The rocks clicked as if whoever it was had huge nails in his shoes. Marly wished she could shrink away like Alice did in Wonderland so she could hide behind one of those cheeses or behind a stone. Anywhere—

The footsteps stopped. Absolute stillness. Marly held her breath and noticed Joe's deep, steady breathing close beside her. A squirrel ran past the door, which stood half open, then came back and glanced in, and ran off again.

After a long time Marly whispered, "Where did he go? Did he go away?"

She saw Joe swallow. The steps coming were not nearly as bad as the silence since they stopped. Joe looked up as if searching for a window or a crack in the walls, but there weren't any. The only light came from the door. Marly knew why he looked. He felt as she did, as if they were being watched. They waited again. Nothing! Then Joe whispered, "I'll look . . ." and moved carefully to the door.

He jumped back. She had never seen that look on Joe's

face before. "He's standing there, watching. He knows we're here," he said. For once Joe was whispering.

It wasn't at all like Joe not to just walk out and say something. He talked to policemen and bus-drivers and everybody. Marly felt as if her blood had stopped running in her veins. She was shivering all over and still held the dipper in her hand.

"The thing to do is just slip out—and then—"

"What?"

"Then *run*. Marly, he's got a huge cane." He looked at her. "Can you really run fast for once?"

She wasn't even sure she could move, let alone run. But she nodded. What else could she do? "Oh, Joe, we shouldn't have come and looked like this . . ." she whispered.

Joe slid toward the door again, beckoning for her to follow. "Now I'll jump out and start down the hill and you come on after, as fast as you can. Don't look up the steps, or anywhere. Just run," he said.

She felt paralyzed. But she found that she could move. She slid after Joe along the cold drippy stone wall, so close she touched him. He got to the door, and she heard him take a deep breath.

Then he leaped out into the sun and ran. She went after him, stumbling and running and half falling down the next steps, which went to a little dam, and then streaking over the meadow.

The hermit shouted after them. At the bottom of the meadow they went under the wire fence. For the first time, then, Marly dared to glance back. There he was, a tall thin bearded man. He was halfway down the steps. He was waving his arms, and he had the strangest thing she ever

saw over his shoulders—a kind of yoke, with a bucket hang-ing on each end. He looked like a gigantic eagle with its wings spread. In one hand was a cane.

"He was going after water and heard us in there, I guess," Joe said. "Come on!"

On their own road, Joe said he hadn't really been scared. It was only that you couldn't tell about people like that. "You hear such queer things. In the newspapers there are all those awful stories, like that old man who went into that trailer in New Mexico." He kept glancing back. "If I'd been alone, I'd have just talked to him. Fritz says he's a queer old man but nice when you know him." He stopped in the road. "Maybe we shouldn't have run like that," he said.

"Joe, we couldn't just stay and have him come in after us. We couldn't!"

"It didn't seem like we could, did it?" Joe looked awfully bothered. "Until after, I didn't think of anything else we could do. But now . . ." He stood still. "I'm about to go back, Marly. That was a dumb thing to do—just run-ning like that. I was thinking about you." His voice ac-cused her. "Why do you always have to follow along?"

"You would too have run! You were just as scared as I was, and you know it! Besides, it was all your fault, going around looking at everything the way you did. Why, maybe he was right there in his house when you kept looking in!"

"That note on the box said he was gone," Joe said.

"It didn't say what day he was gone, did it? And it didn't say when he was coming back."

He looked at her angrily. "Why didn't you think of that before?" He didn't like the idea of himself peering through that screen, practically right into the face of the hermit himself.

"I'm going back and apologize," he said.

"Joe! Now? By yourself?"

"Well, you don't need to come!"

"I didn't mean I wanted to. I only thought maybe you'd better go back with Fritz or somebody. Joe—the thing to do is to get *introduced*—"

He looked uncertain. But then he started walking toward home again. "Maybe so," he said.

Goodness, boys were funny! She didn't blame Joe in the least for being scared—who wouldn't be?—and she didn't mind saying she was scared either. But she knew that if she should mention one word about the way they ran out of that springhouse and down the hill, he would hate her for a week, if not forever. She wanted to tell it, making it as gruesome as she could, but she knew Joe would never forgive her if she so much as mentioned it. For the millionth time, she was glad she wasn't a boy. It was all right for girls to be scared or silly or even ask dumb questions. Everybody just laughed and thought it was funny. But if anybody caught Joe asking a dumb question or even thought he was the littlest bit scared, he went red and purple and white. Daddy was even something like that, as old as he was.

At their own lane she said, "Joe, I don't blame you one little bit for being scared. Honest, I—"

"Just shut up about it, can't you?" he said.

She had to hang onto her tongue so hard it practically ached. She actually had to hold the tip with her teeth to keep from telling, especially when Joe went out to work with Daddy at the weeding, and she and Mother were alone with the dishes. Once she started to say, "This morning Joe and I—" and stopped and bit her tongue.

"Did you see Chrissie this morning? She didn't feel a bit well last night," Mother said.

"No. We didn't." If she told this time, Marly thought, she'd never get to go anywhere with Joe again as long as she lived. It was a relief to finish the dishes and go up to her room and shut the door. She read all afternoon so she wouldn't go down and tell. And when it was time to help with supper, Joe was in the kitchen, washing.

He looked at her, hard. "I'll bet a cow you told Mother all about it," he said.

"I didn't! So!"

"Didn't what?" Daddy asked, coming in.

"What you'll do this time is tell on yourself," Marly said to Joe in a whisper, and giggled.

"I'm going over to see Fritz after supper," Joe said.

But as it turned out, he didn't. And Marly didn't have to worry about telling that story any more, because the only other person in the world to know it, besides her and Joe, came to call right after supper and told it himself.

You could have "knocked Joe down with a canary feather," as Mr. Chris would say it. When the knock came, Joe happened to answer. He stood there, staring. He actually forgot to say, "Come in." Daddy stood up from his chair and took his pipe out of his mouth and said, "Hello! Come in, come in."

When the hermit came in, the whole room was suddenly absolutely thick with the smell of goats, just like Chrissie said. He didn't look very different from any elderly man, close to, and had a clipped gray beard and his coat buttoned all the way down the front. His hair looked quite combed, and he was tall and thin and carried the same cane he had waved from the steps that morning.

"Good evening," he said.

He sounded polite and special, the way he spoke, not wild in the least, in spite of the wild goat smell all around him. "I went to ask Mr. Chris where the children lived," he said. "I'm afraid I frightened them away." He looked straight at Joe and then at Marly. "I did not know who it was, in my springhouse. I thought it was some bad boys who have come, sometimes, to steal my cheeses. Even, once, they dropped every cheese and poured all my milk into the spring."

Mother and Daddy glanced at each other, and at Joe, and at Marly, questioning.

"In the spring? What did they do that for?" Marly cried. "Why, it's a *lovely* spring—"

"Were you at his place, Joe? You and Marly?" Daddy asked. "I wondered what you two had been up to today."

The hermit spoke again, quickly, and held out a package in his hand, wrapped in newspaper. "Nothing was harmed," he said. "It is all right. I hope they will come again." He was looking at Mother, and Mother moved to him and took the package from his hand.

"I brought some of my own cheese and honey," he said. "Very good. There is no goat cheese like this except in Switzerland, where I came from as a boy."

"Thank you very much," Mother said.

"If the children will come again tomorrow, I will show them how it is I make the cheese," he said.

"And the chains?" Joe spoke for the first time, eagerly, relieved. "Fritz said you showed him how you make those wooden chains."

The hermit laughed. His teeth were long and brown, but his laugh was beautiful, Marly thought. It sounded pleased. "The chains, they are simple!" he said. "If you have wood and a good knife, I will show you now. Tonight."

Mother glanced at Daddy. Marly knew she was wondering whether Daddy would want this goat-man to stay. He used to object to people coming and staying, especially queer old people who talked and talked. Mother knew all sorts of people wherever she went, it seemed, and they often came to call while Daddy was away.

"Please sit down," Daddy said. "Joe, that one knife we sharpened—"

Whoever would have thought that morning of the hermit sitting that very night in their very own kitchen? He took an ordinary stick of kindling from the box and smelled it and said, "Maple. Good!" and proceeded to make a neat little totem pole out of it. He worked quickly with long, stained fingers. Miraculously the first link appeared, and the second, and the third. He kept having Joe do some of the work, to learn. Joe worked slowly, his mouth pursed up.

"It is rough, this, to show you. It should be done carefully," the hermit said. He stayed for four solid hours! Before the chain was finished, Mother made a big pot of coffee. She let it boil and boil, and it drove some of the goat smell out of the house.

When he went away, the hermit said, "Promise to come back soon. The Father and the Mother, too." He looked at Marly. "I have a telescope. Mr. Chris said you will like to see through it. Not stars only. Small things everywhere. From my hill"—he smiled—"I get acquainted with all the ducks on the pond."

Joe said, not looking at Mother or at Daddy, "I'm sorry I looked into your house the way I did. I thought . . ."

Marly wondered if Joe was going to tell the truth, that he thought the hermit was away. But he didn't. His voice hung in the air, and the hermit said, "When I am not there, come in and make yourself at home. I am sometimes at the barn, in the woods perhaps, or at the hives." He looked at Daddy. "For a time my own son lived with me here on the mountain," he said. "Now he is gone to be a soldier."

As he went off, Joe sat on the step and watched. For a long time he just sat there, swinging the chain in his hand.

"What on earth will we do with this awful cheese?" Mother said. "Phew! It's strong!"

Joe stood up and went in. He looked just the way Daddy used to look when he was absolutely furious. "It's wonderful cheese!" he said. "And he's a wonderful old man! I'm going to learn how to make cheese and chains and everything and get me a house and live *just like him*."

He went tramping up the stairs.

"Well!" Daddy said.

9 A BIG DECISION

The summer world grew and swelled and ripened. Weeds along the edges of the fields and in the rail-fence corners were up to Marly's waist. By the Fourth of July they were beginning to go brown, and Daddy warned Joe and Marly not to toss their sparkler wires too far with the wires hot. At the celebration in town, ice cream dripped before you could get your cone licked even once around. *That* was really summer.

"Summer," Mr. Chris said that night after the fireworks were over and they were all having homemade ice cream on his front porch, "is fruit time mostly, just the way spring is mostly flower time." Marly could see that it was true. For the rest of the summer it seemed to get truer and truer. Every flower that had bloomed bore some kind of seed or fruit, and it was a surprise to see how the different ones turned out. For instance, the greeny-looking clintonia flower bells became beautiful blue berries, but there were so few of those you could search the whole woods and not find enough to string a bracelet. Rose hips were everywhere, yellow and red, and you could make strings of beads clear to your toes without stirring off the porch. Lily of the valley bore clusters of brightest red; but the false lily of the

valley in the woods had berries that were speckled with
brown. Solomon's-seal had dark blue berries in a neat row
where the flowers had hung under the leaves. It was as if
all its little bells had run away and forgotten their clappers.
The large pale flowers of the May apple had dropped their
petals, and their middles swelled bigger and bigger; Chrissie
said she'd pay a good price for a basket to make preserves,
but it was hard to find so much as a pintful on account of
the animals liking them so well.

Where trillium had spread its wide white petals, there
were now long beads of berries, some red and some black.
Twisted-stalk had baubles, little transparent red berries
you could see into. Mr. Chris said Dutchman's-breeches
had such bad fruit for cows to eat that their summer name
was "little blue staggers."

Joe and Marly did so much berrying, what with straw-
berries and then red raspberries and then blackberries, that
Joe said he was absolutely berried-out. But they kept going.
Fritz showed them such special blackberry patches that
they could fill a quart without taking a single step, and
each berry was the size of Mr. Chris's thumb. Every time,
too, there was apt to be pie afterwards. And with blueberries or huckleberries, there might be pie and then muf-
fins for breakfast besides and maybe pudding for lunch.

For a while chokecherries were thick on the trees along
the lumber roads that had been a mist of white blooms
earlier. They meant jelly. So did elderberries, later.

Eat—eat—eat! Not only the wild things but all the things
in Daddy's garden got ready for eating about the same
time, until Mother said she felt food running out of her
ears. She canned and canned and juiced and juiced and
sent lots of things to a freezer so they could be used on

week ends during winter visits. "I feel like Joseph in Egypt getting ready for the lean years during the fat years," she said.

In August Marly found the oddest berry she had ever seen. Mr. Chris had warned her "never to eat strangers," so she carried a big spray of these to ask him about. Each berry sat on a cunning scarlet flower which was left behind when the berry was picked away.

"Pokeberries," Mr. Chris said. "Are *they* ready already? We always made ink out of them for school."

He said she could taste them if she wanted to. And of course she did—once. But she'd as soon drink ink for breakfast.

When Mother saw them, she laughed and said, "Grandma called them inkberries. She was always sorry to see them starting to ripen. They were a sign it was almost time for us to go home again, back to school."

Marly gathered a whole lot of them and made a little dish of ink. Mother said she'd never in her life seen such a big fuss over such a little juice. A whole summer of jellying and juicing, she said, hadn't made so much mess in the kitchen. Purple stains were absolutely everywhere, on the ceiling and even in drawers that had been a little open. But there was enough in the dish, finally to write almost a half-page of a letter to Carol. "Imagine—a *pokeberry* letter!" Marly said. "That's as nice as strawberry bouquets."

The carpets of wintergreen began to show red berries, and Mr. Chris said they'd not stop growing all winter long. "Lost people have been known to brush away the snow and eat those berries to save their lives," he said.

The thick green leaves tasted just like chewing gum.

Chrissie served for dessert one night what she said was the "best berry-combination in the whole world"—wintergreen berries and blueberries. Marly didn't say so, but raspberries and currants seemed better to her.

The creatures in the drying ponds sang louder every night; the creatures in the grass and in the fields sang louder every day! Mr. Chris said they knew winter was coming soon, and they had to get all the noise out of their systems.

Then a few leaves drifted down. Winged seeds lay beneath the tulip trees, and all along the roads milkweed pods began to spill white silky threads.

The days seemed to go faster and faster. Mr. Chris looked sad. One night he looked up at the sky and said in the saddest voice Marly had ever heard from him, "When the moon comes full again, there'll be a killing frost."

Chrissie looked sad too. "I wish you could see the leaves turn, Lee," she said again and again. "After you go, I won't be able to stand looking in this direction at night. It's been so good to have somebody in this house, watching for the light in the evening just the way I did when your grandma was here."

Three weeks—then two weeks until time for school. It seemed odd to Marly how sudden it seemed after the whole summer. Summer looked like forever in front of you, and now it was almost gone. She hated the thought of leaving Maple Hill so much that she even hated the boxes Mother started to pack in. But Joe whistled as he brought them down. He didn't seem to care much about anything, Marly thought.

One day when she was coming downstairs she heard Daddy say something mysterious and important. She could tell from the sound of his voice how important it was.

"Well, we can't go on postponing it any longer, can we? *We've got to decide now!*" he said.

"I expect Marly would be glad," Mother said. "But I don't know about Joe."

"I didn't even think we could get in and out," Daddy said. "But Chris says with a good load of that gravel on the low place, we wouldn't have a bit of trouble. The county keeps the roads clear for the school bus."

Marly felt herself beginning to tremble, because she was beginning to know what they were talking about. "Every objection I think of, Chris figures a way out," Daddy went on. "They really do want us to stay."

Stay! Here? At Maple Hill? *All winter?* Marly was listening so hard that her ears felt like a donkey's, on either side. Mother was clattering the skillet, and it was hard to hear every word she said.

". . . as tight as ever, isn't it? After all, Grandma stayed here all the year round as far back as I can remember—and before. And as Chris says, if we got the heat in . . . It's not the house that worries me, Dale."

"I know." Marly heard the sadness in Daddy's voice. "It's not fair for the children. If it wasn't for school . . ."

"Of course, I don't see anything wrong with country schools myself. The children get lots more attention than they do in those crowded city schools now. It's only that Joe was so pleased about being in such a big school, so new and everything, and he likes his crowd. And he wanted to get a horn and play in the band."

Marly hardly heard past the words "country schools." She and Joe had seen the little Maple Mountain school. It looked just like a church, with a funny bell-tower. It even had a graveyard behind it, on a low hill, with the stones overgrown and tumbling. They traced interesting names on some of them, like Mehitable and Josephus, and even grue-some verses about dying. When they looked through the dusty windows of the schoolhouse, they laughed and laughed. There were rows of pictures still pinned to the walls, birds and pussy willows and tulips that the children had colored in the spring. And there was the hugest, round-est stove they ever saw in all their lives. Six rows of desks went from a little tiny row to a great big row. Joe said it looked like a school for "the six bears"—from the little bears to the big bears.

"Imagine having to go to a school like that!" he said.

What was Joe going to think? She couldn't wait to tell him and find out. She crept upstairs again and into Joe's room, but he was still asleep. He looked tall when he was lying down, especially because he spread himself every direction. And once he was spread on the mattress, he didn't move; Daddy said he slept like a stone and a log rolled together.

"Joe!" she said.

He growled and turned over and pulled the covers nearly over his head.

She sat on the edge of the bed. It'd be fun to tease him about that funny school, she thought. So she leaned down close to his ear and said: "Joe—guess what! We're not ever going back to Pittsburgh, we're going to stay right here at Maple Hill *all winter long!*"

"*What?*" He sat up so fast she almost fell off the edge of the bed. You'd have thought he hadn't been asleep for a week.

"Yes—I just now heard Mother and Daddy talking. He said it's a good enough house to stay in all winter, and Mr.

Chris says we can get in and out, and Mother says the school bus comes by, and we get to go to that funny little old school by the graveyard!" Her words came tumbling over each other, and it came to Marly as she said them that they weren't strictly true, at least not yet. But then she had never yet known something Daddy wanted not to be what Mother wanted too. And anybody could tell from the way he talked that he wanted to stay at Maple Hill.

Joe looked absolutely horrified. *"That school?"* She could see on his face the thought of the beautiful school where he would go in Pittsburgh. A solid block of buildings with rooms and rooms and a gymnasium and everything, with policemen to help all the children across the streets.

"I don't believe it," he said, and got out of bed and started for the door.

"Joe—" Marly hurried after him. "Mother and Daddy were talking, see. And I don't think it's all settled, but Daddy—"

"I knew it wasn't so," Joe said. "You always get things wrong." He stood and looked at her angrily. "I'll bet you made the whole thing up. Why, we started packing yesterday."

"I heard them," she said. "Mother said she didn't see anything wrong with country schools. I heard her—"

"Honest?"

"Honest. Daddy said it wouldn't be fair for us, and she said she didn't see anything wrong—"

"Imagine!" Joe interrupted her as if he couldn't stand to hear another word. "That school! All those little kids right in the same room. Why, I wouldn't go to that school if there wasn't another school in the whole world! Why—"

He didn't seem able to find even the words to say how awful the whole idea was. He turned and opened the door, but Marly caught his arm.

"Joe." Marly made her face go as long and solemn as she could. "I know how Mother feels. You see, Daddy's better here, isn't he?"

For a minute Joe stood looking at her. She saw his face get afraid, just the way it used to get when Daddy was cross. Once Daddy even reached out and slapped Joe's face, hard, and Mother hurried and took hold of Daddy's arm and said, "Don't you dare!" Joe looked just the same now as he had then.

"The other day when Mother and I were in the garden," Marly said, "Daddy was at the other end of the row. And Mother said, 'Isn't it wonderful how much better Daddy is at Maple Hill?' He was laughing and talking and telling stories and singing the whole time, all the time it took to pick the last of the beans and pull all those carrots and beets."

While she talked, Joe walked slowly back to his bed. He lay down and pulled the covers up again. The huge movie theaters, the museums, the concerts, the science exhibits. She knew all the things Joe loved about the city. He liked the bridges and the hills and even the steel mills. He liked noise and people and policemen. He had his crowd, and they went all kinds of places together. Cities were lots better for boys, she thought, even boys who liked to explore.

"Don't you like Maple Hill, Joe?" she asked. "Not a bit?"

"Sure I do." His voice sounded lost and little, deep in the covers. "But . . ." His face came out. "Why, I was going to get that horn and play in the band and everything."

"Joe, maybe we're not really going to stay here," she said.

"You just tell Daddy how you feel. They were just saying we'd have to decide."

He sat up again. "How do you mean, Marly? I thought you meant it was all settled."

"They were just talking, see, and Daddy said we had to decide."

He threw the covers off so hard they went all over the floor. "Well, I'm going down and find out," he said. "First you say one thing, and then you say the other. If you don't *know* something, you just ought to shut up about it." He was on the stairs already. "I'm going down and find out," he said again.

Marly heard Daddy say, "Find out what?"

"Oh, dear," she thought. Why did she get excited and make out that things were so when they weren't? At least not yet. She was always saying things were settled, and then sometimes they were, and sometimes they weren't. She followed Joe down the stairs, wishing she hadn't said a single word.

"Are we going to stay here all winter and have to go to that funny old school, like Marly says?" Joe demanded.

Mother turned from the stove. "Did Marly say that?" she asked. "How in the world did she get hold of that idea?"

Joe turned accusingly as Marly came into the kitchen. She said, feeling her face go hot, "I heard you talking about it. I was just coming downstairs and I—"

"Come and sit down, both of you," Daddy said. He looked at Mother. "I told you we'd better settle it, Lee. Well, now's the time."

Poor Joe's face had the struggle on it again. He didn't look at Marly at all. If Daddy was going to say he was well here and sick somewhere else, what would there be to settle?

"Marly was in too big a hurry, as usual," Daddy said. "We haven't decided, because, after all, there are four of us, and this is a mighty big decision."

So during breakfast and for a long time afterward, they talked it over. Daddy got an old score-card and crossed out *Them* and *Us* and wrote "Points for Staying" and "Points for Going." But this wasn't like cards at all, where the same number on each side makes people tied. Some points were more important than others, so that the one point Mother made—"Daddy is better at Maple Hill"—would have canceled out forty points on the other side. Everybody knew that the whole time. When Daddy wrote that one down, he looked as miserable as could be.

"Now, remember, all of you, that's no more important than Schools and Advantages on the other side," he said. But there was so much on the Maple Hill side, it was really ridiculous—like "Live cheaper in the country" and "The Chrises" and "Could live on government pension without Mother working." Marly thought of suggesting "Miracles" for that side, but she was afraid they wouldn't know just what she meant. She wasn't sure, either, that she could explain.

By the time they voted, even Joe could see that the city didn't have a chance in the world. It was as if he could see his trumpet and his fine big school go floating away. But he was a good sport, Joe, as always. He actually voted to stay, even though his throat wobbled in the middle, and he went outside right after and disappeared down the road. She wondered if he'd cry when he was alone; she would have. But she guessed he wouldn't.

Daddy stood in the kitchen door, watching him go. "It's only for this year," he said. "Then I'll be ready to go back to my old job. I know it."

Marly wanted to run after Joe and tell him what Daddy had said. But she decided to wait. If he *should* happen to cry, he wouldn't want anybody barging right into the middle of it.

So she just ran down to the Chrises to tell them what the big decision was. Nobody wanted to cry about it there! Mr. Chris picked her up and tossed her around, laughing. Chrissie said, "Chris, be careful!" but she laughed, too. They began talking about all the marvelous things that happened in winter on Maple Mountain, and how perfect Thanksgiving was, and Christmas, and how Marly and Joe could have a horse to pull that cunning little sleigh. "Joe can paint it red like it used to be," Mr. Chris said, "and I'll get out our old sleigh-bells. You folks will think you've walked right into a Christmas card!"

"I'll tell Joe about the sleigh," Marly said. "He feels so bad about that funny school."

They both looked at her, surprised. Mr. Chris's face went redder, even, than it usually looked. "Why, that's a fine school," he said. "We've got as good a school as any in this country, I can tell you. And big, too. Growing all the time."

Marly was puzzled at first, but then it turned out that Joe wouldn't go to the little school by the graveyard at all. He was twelve, so he would go on the bus to town. "Do they have a band?" she asked eagerly.

"A band? I'll tell the world they've got a band! If Joe wants to be in a band, he'll like that one, all right. They march at all the football games in red and gold suits, and last year they went to a state contest and won honorable mention!"

Marly was so eager to tell Joe about the school and the band that she ran all the way home. But Joe wasn't there. He didn't even come back for lunch at noon.

"Do you know, I wouldn't be surprised if he went to see his friend, the hermit?" Daddy said. "Isn't it the oddest thing, the way Joe took to that old man?" Daddy sounded the least bit jealous, Marly thought.

"Joe helps with the bees and the goats, and they're building a wonderful fence," Marly said.

"I wish he'd come home and eat, at least," Mother said, looking out of the window and down the hill at the empty road.

"There are worse things than goat cheese and honey," Daddy said. "Chris says Harry bakes the best rye bread he ever ate."

When the dishes were done, Marly slipped away and walked to Harry's place. Clear from the second turn, she could see that Joe was there. He and Harry were building a little fence of sharp poles clear around the house, weaving it together with willow boughs that crissed and crossed and wound together. Joe had told Marly about that fence. It was just like the kind the Mexican Indians made, he said, only they made theirs out of cactus that went right on blooming with bright red flowers. Harry said his fence would take root in places, maybe, and get green leaves on it in the spring.

Joe saw her coming, and before she could say a word about the school or the band or anything, he was shouting news of his own. "Marly—guess what? I'm going to take two goats home for the winter!"

"Joe! Why, Mother won't—"

"Why won't she let me?" he interrupted angrily. "If we're going to live in the country, we've got to figure how to manage. Harry's showing me how to milk and separate and make butter and cheese and everything. Do you think I'm tramping all the way to Chris's place for milk all winter?"

Harry was sitting on the ground, cutting a neat sharp end on each of a pile of fence sticks. He looked up at Marly, and his gray beard shook when he laughed. "Joe is right," he said. "You must have everything you need, all together, before the winter really begins. For you I have something, too, and Joe will make a fence like this for them to run— but much higher."

It was chickens. Harry said he had too many, and they must take at least eight home now, today. For a present, he had already prepared an old orange crate to carry them in, tied with neat rope handles at either end. "For these you will be caretaker," Harry said to Marly. "Each on a farm should care for something alive and useful."

Marly had never dared look at Harry very closely for very long. But now she looked right straight at his eyes. They were very sharp and blue, but very kind and twinkling.

It was the queerest thing, but Marly actually got so excited about the goats and chickens that she forgot about telling Joe what she had come to tell. She had never really seen part of Harry's place, and now Joe showed her everything. Down the ravine, west of the hill above the spring-house, Harry had built three wonderful little dams. They were made of large flat stones piled close together. They were beautiful, like fine stone walls, with grass and moss growing over them. All around his house were small square

116

patches of things enclosed in fences to keep the rabbits out, and—as Harry said—to keep the flowers and vegetables in. In front of the door were patches of zinnias and marigolds and rhubarb.

The place where he chopped wood was nice. It was under the hugest oak tree Marly had even seen in all her life. There was a sawhorse, and there were three different-sized woodpiles, one of big pieces, one of middle-sized pieces, and one of little pieces for kindlings, all ranked perfectly. The strange yoke Harry had worn that first day was lying against the tree. He had carved it out of a smaller tree, he said, and it fitted his shoulders neatly. It was covered with nice designs. Everything possible was carved with designs, even the stanchions where the goats put their heads and the stalls in the little barn. There was an odd little stand where they leaped to be milked. And every single goat had a name out of Shakespeare!

"We're getting Rosalind and Audrey," Joe said.

Wooden chains were everywhere, from a huge one with links as round as Marly's head to a tiny one Harry was using for a bookmark in his Bible.

As the sun went down, Harry took her to the head of the meadow to look through his telescope. He had it trained on the pond below where ducks were swimming. "Any day now the black ducks come," he said, "and the mallards. Then we will have good meat." He could turn the glass on the meadow, too, and watch pheasants coming and going. Marly could hardly tear her eyes away. Looking through that long tube at a pheasant made you feel as if you were taking a walk with him. She could see his white collar and the white tufts of his ears, and the sun shining on him as it went lower and lower showed dozens of colors clear down to the tip of his long pointed tail.

Harry smiled when she drew back at last, sighing. "Sometimes, can you imagine, people ask me if I am lonely here!" he said.

It did seem a very silly question. He had six goats and five hives of bees and a flock of chickens and a herd of geese and a pair of cardinals that stayed near his house the whole year around. He had rabbits that came to eat from his hands and deer that walked down to drink at his dams every morning and never ran off when he talked to them. He had woodchucks and a coon and squirrels and chipmunks. He had an owl in his barn who talked to him at night and a pair of swallows. He had pheasants and grouse and the ducks down on the pond and fishes behind all his dams. And peepers and frogs—not to mention spiders having thousands of babies in his windows. He showed her one spider with four sacks of eggs swinging right over his table where he could watch her while he ate. Then if you considered moths and butterflies and beetles . . . "And lizards and efts," Joe said.

"And the sparrows are always here," Harry said.

"And snakes," said Joe, just because he knew Marly was scared of them. But then he added quickly, "Marly, wait until you know the goats. You'll agree they're the best."

It was true, as he said, that every face of every goat was different—as different as people. Each one was sure to look straight into your eyes, though, so they were alike about being curious. There were three little half-grown goats, and it was nice and comical to see how much they loved Harry. They tried to get close to him for a rubbing when he went into the barn and stretched and bleated for a little touch on the nose. When he let them out, they leaped and ran and climbed onto every bump in the meadow, gazing around from every little height as if they owned the world.

"Do you know, Marly, Harry lived in a city *for fifty years?*" Joe asked. "This morning when I came over, he told me."

Harry heard. "It was because of Mr. Chris I stayed here," he said. "I was tired and sick of the world, and my wife had left me in disgust. I had been fighting in the war and then in the streets at home, and even in my own house. I was as sick of fighting as Joe says your father is. So one day I put my belongings into a sack and started to walk like a tramp. One morning I came along this road. I was thinking hard thoughts about all men, and I was hungry. Then suddenly I saw this man working in a field. Right there, below where the dam is. I stopped and we began to talk together."

Harry gazed down toward the pond and over the green valley with fields of cabbages blue in squares and meadows going brown here and there. "The first thing I thought," Harry said, "was, 'This man looks like a tree.' He seemed to stand with his legs planted in the ground."

"That's just what I thought!" Marly said in triumph.

"Such things happen in the old stories," Harry said, laughing. "Maybe he really is a tree. I asked whether he needed help with any of his work, for I needed to earn my supper. So I stayed that night. And it turned out that he needed help all winter long. His hired man had gone away. After a year, he gave me this house to live in, and I have bought this little piece of the mountain around it."

Did everything good go back somehow to Mr. Chris? Marly wondered. He had found the first pair of goats for

Harry and had provided the first chickens. "He never told us a word about doing that for you," Marly said.

"When you have done a great many good things, you forget to speak of them," Harry said. "It is those who do very little who must talk of it." He still stood gazing down toward the road, toward Mr. Chris's fine big house. "I became too old to be of much help on his place," he said. "But I wanted to stay here and live, so I sent for my books and my knives. Soon it will be twenty years I have lived

here on this same hill. It is exactly as the great Thoreau said: 'Why should I explore the world when there is so much to explore between that road and my own doorstep?' "

It was a strange procession that went along the road at sunset. Harry drove the two goats, on whose necks he had hung garlands of goldenrod and wild aster to make it "a royal procession." Both goats and the hermit himself carried loads of fence sticks for Joe to build his chicken-run. Joe and Marly carried the crate of chickens between them,

trying not to jar them too much from one side to another. Even so, they squawked the whole way, poking their heads out of the cracks to complain.

Whatever will Mother think? And Daddy? Just as Marly expected, they came out of the house when they heard the procession coming. There they stood, gazing down the hill. It was not until then that Marly remembered about the band and the school.

"Joe—Mr. Chris says I go to the little school, but you don't. You go to town, to a great big school where they have a huge band that wears gold and red and wins prizes— and marches in parades!"

He hardly seemed to hear. He was beaming as Harry drove his Rosalind and Audrey into the dooryard. "Harry's going to make a speech," he said.

And Harry did. He stood with his wrinkled old hat held in front of him like a man presenting flowers to a great lady. "My father used to tell me that in his country when there were neighbors come to remain," he said, "milk was brought for their supper and eggs for their breakfast. Now that you have made this great decision to stay at Maple Hill, we have brought gifts to show that we are glad."

Mother was too amazed to speak. Daddy didn't manage anything but "Well, well, well!" which wasn't much of a speech. But the goats began to bleat happily, and the chickens talked all together.

"Do you want to see me milk?" Joe asked.

Actually, Joe could make milk come spurting into the bucket. Mother looked at Daddy, and Marly could practically read her mind: "Do you think if we stay in the country, Joe is going to have many of these queer friends?" But Daddy could hardly keep his eyes off Joe.

"Mr. Harry," he said suddenly, "do you think you could stay for supper?"

Joe was awfully pleased. But Marly couldn't help being rather glad when Harry said he had to hurry home to milk his goats and feed his chickens and geese, because Mother really looked a little sick.

Joe noticed, too. When Harry had gone he said to Mother, "You just wait until you know him, Mother. He's the most wonderful man in the world."

"Next to Mr. Chris," Marly said.

She and Joe had the thought at the same minute, and said, right together, "Next to Daddy." Then they linked their little fingers, the way you do when you've said something both together, and made wishes. The wishes have to be secret, but Marly knew from Joe's look that his was about the big decision. And so was hers.

10 JOE DOES A CHRISTMAS THING

You would think Maple Mountain was on fire.

In every direction the trees were red and yellow. When the sun struck them suddenly, flying through windy clouds, the brightness was almost more than Marly could bear. The redness seemed to come from inside each tree in a wonderful way; it was the red she saw through her hand when she held it against the sun. The yellowness glistened like golden hair, and the wind shook it, and bits of gold spun down upon the grass.

What a lovely world! Every morning on Maple Hill, Marly woke in the very middle of a scarlet and golden miracle.

"This is the best time of the year," she said to Mr. Chris.

He shook his head. "It's too short, Marly," he said. "And it means winter is just around the corner. To me spring is the best time." He sounded sad, she thought. How could anybody be sad in such a world?

The little schoolhouse stood among red maples. The first thing the teacher had the children do was draw maple leaves. Marly was glad it was something easy, because she wanted to look around at the other children. It was strange to be in the very same room with first graders and sixth graders and all the graders between. In Marly's own class were only three boys and two girls. "Well, now that we have Marly, it is evened up," the teacher said. "The boys will have to behave themselves."

She was jolly and fat. Her name was Miss Perkinsen, which had a gay sound, Marly thought. She was the busiest person Marly had ever seen in all her life. Imagine, having to know everything that six grades must know. Every month a bookmobile drove into the schoolyard. The driver was a beautiful red-headed girl, and she left piles and piles of books.

At first Joe didn't tell much about his school. He was slow to make friends, and he missed his gang in the city. But in two weeks he got off the bus one day with a shining horn. He ran all the way up the hill and hardly got his books down when he began to blow. The band leader at his school had given him one lesson already, and he had a little book to look at. He blew and blew and *blew* until Mother said the roof would fly off before suppertime.

"Here we came to the country to be *quiet!*" Daddy said. But he laughed when he said it, and when Joe finished blowing at last (long enough to eat), Daddy took the horn and tried blowing it himself. His cheeks went out and his face got red, and he didn't make a sound. Joe had to show him how.

He showed Marly, too. Then he blew again until Mother said he absolutely had to go to bed. The band leader had told him if he learned to blow right away he could march in the band the very next Saturday.

And he actually did.

There was a parade in town on account of the Fair, and all of them went. Everybody in Marly's school went and all the people who lived for miles in every direction. Everybody in the whole county went to that Fair, and everybody took the very best of everything he had made or raised that year. It was the most beautiful thing Marly had ever seen—except for the country itself. Mr. Chris took a huge pumpkin and a huge ear of corn and a bunch of cornstalks that touched the ceiling in the high exhibit room. Mrs. Chris took canned corn and peaches and cherries and lots of jelly of different kinds and a wonderful big white cake. Marly was proud to notice how many blue ribbons the Chrises got, and one or two red ones besides. Mrs. Chris also took a big bouquet of her chrysanthemums, golden colored and as big as dinner plates. Mr. Chris made a tongue twister about "Chrissie's Chrysanthemums."

There was a Ferris wheel at the Fair and a merry-go-round and all kinds of booths and games and things to eat. But the best part of the whole thing was the parade with Joe marching in it.

Marly had never before noticed how handsome Joe was. He had a cocky little hat and colored ropes over his shoulders. Goodness! When she saw him lift the horn to play, she was worried. Of course she didn't say so, but she was afraid Joe's blowings might spoil the whole band. But his noises mixed in with all the rest of the noises, so it didn't matter. All the blowings and beatings together sounded wonderful. Joe blew and marched and blew and marched as if he'd done it every day of his life.

When he marched past, Marly and Mother and Daddy and the Chrises and Fritz all began to clap. He went red in the face, but turned and grinned as he passed, and then started to blow again.

The next thing Marly liked best about the Fair was the

place where the animals were. Everybody brought his best animals, too, and his best birds, and some of the boys and girls stayed right by the stalls to sleep. A girl at Marly's school had two beautiful calves she had raised herself, and she polished them up and combed them and washed them as if they were children going to Sunday school. And they won a lovely blue ribbon and a gold one besides.

The horse-pulling was more exciting than the Ferris wheel. Marly had never seen such huge horses in all her life. Then there were ponies and lovely cows like the ones she had had so much trouble with (she walked close beside Daddy in that barn!) and the hugest geese and ducks and odd-looking chickens with crests on their heads and their heels.

And rabbits. And pigs. And everything. Daddy kept saying, "Well, Lee, we haven't even *started* to be farmers yet, have we?"

Mr. Chris said the people with the best jobs at the Fair were the judges who got to taste all the cakes and pies and loaves of bread and cookies and everything. But Mrs. Chris said the nicest thing was the gymnasium where the flower show was. It was like a huge indoor garden.

The whole Fair was at Joe's school, and you'd have thought he owned everything himself when he went around with them after the parade.

Marly heard Mother say to Daddy: "Thank goodness Joe is happy at that school."

Whenever Marly told anything about *her* school during those first weeks, Joe acted quite superior and smarty. But she didn't care. Next year she'd be going on the big yellow bus right along with him. And just now she wouldn't trade jolly Miss Perkinsen and the red-headed book-lady for all the teachers in the whole world and all the horns to blow besides. So there!

Besides, there was Margie.

She lived three miles down the road, and right away she and Marly were friends. Their names were so nearly twin names that they decided it was a sure sign of something special. The very first Saturday after the Fair they made a leaf house on the hill, with a red room and a yellow room and piles of leaves for chairs and davenports and tables. By then the leaves were beginning to fall more every day, and some of the trees had begun to show their skeletons, twiggy and brown. It was a surprise to find that the trees along the road were black walnuts. They cracked some for

Mother, and pretty soon she sent out fresh cookies and milk.

The next Saturday they made another house at Margie's, on a long flat lawn. Margie's mother sent out chocolate cake.

The next Saturday was Margie's birthday party, and Marly gave her a friendship ring. It was Mother's idea. So Margie brought another friendship ring to school the next week, and they decided to be bosom friends for the rest of their lives.

Margie had three big brothers instead of one, and one day in October the whole bunch of them went out mushrooming. Mr. Chris had to check on them, he said, before they could be sent into town to the restaurant man who canned them with a pressure cooker. Mushrooms were terribly dangerous unless you *knew*. There was one called the "destroying angel" that would kill people who ate it so they were absolutely dead in a few days. There were "death cups," too. But then there were lovely and delicious little ones that grew in the meadows where the cows had been. Finding them was like a game of hide and seek, or maybe more like who's-got-the-button. Some were barely out of the ground, lovely and white with a beautiful pink beneath like the spokes of an umbrella. Every single one had a different shape in some way, like people. Every time Marly picked one, she rather expected she'd find that little fairy, Thumbelina, sitting under it.

Joe was right that he could make more money with mushrooms in a few days than he could in a week or so on his paper route in Pittsburgh. But of course the mushrooms only lasted for a little while every year. Mother made mushroom omelet, and they had steak with mushrooms and chicken with mushrooms. Marly was rather glad when Joe came in one morning and said there wasn't another one to be found.

The lovely leaves, too, did not last very long. The trees became more and more bare. She could see bird's nests that she had not dreamed were there. Then, one night in October, it froze. Daddy had been covering his tomato plants every night, and some tomatoes could still be picked in the cool sunshine. But this night left every plant as black, Daddy said, as the Ace of Spades. The whole garden looked stubby and ugly. Mother's zinnias stood sad and brown and rustled like straw in the wind.

Daddy didn't seem to mind about the garden much, because soon it was hunting time. Before, he always had to go a long way to hunt, but now he said he would practically hunt his own game.

Marly did not say so to Daddy, or to Joe either, but she hated hunting season. She hated to come home and see piles of bright pheasant feathers and the long thin dead bodies of the birds—though at supper she forgot and ate and ate and ate. The men talked of nothing but hunting for a while, how they went here and there and missed and hit and how their dogs behaved. Every morning early the sound of guns came through the windows at Maple Hill.

Then it snowed.

The first lazy flakes were coming down one November day when Marly walked to school. They touched the ground and faded away. But more and more kept falling. By night the ground was misty white out of the windows.

In the morning Maple Hill had turned into a different place entirely. First it had been brown, Marly thought, and then all green, and then yellow and gold, and now it was white. If she must choose, which would she choose, she wondered.

She asked Daddy and Mother and Joe which they would choose.

Joe thought it was a silly question to ask, because they didn't have to choose. But Daddy said he chose green because of his nice garden. Mother chose red and yellow.

"Which do you choose, Marly?" Daddy asked.

She looked out of the window. It was fairyland. All the twigs had turned to lace, and the trees were stooped with snow. Suddenly a bright red bird flew into the bush by the window and looked at her. A cardinal! The very one Mr. Chris could talk to, maybe. He had told her to put out food, and the birds would come to the windows all winter long. It was, just that moment, the best miracle of all.

"I choose Now!" she said.

That afternoon she knew she was right. Mr. Chris came over on his sleigh with one of the extra horses hitched behind. And she and Joe brought out that old sleigh in the barn and even found the bells in the harness room. Then they went everywhere, jingling and dashing through the snow the way the people did in that old song, *Jingle Bells*.

If there was anybody who didn't know what month it was, the school windows would tell him. After the colored leaves were taken down, there were pumpkin faces. Then huge turkey cutouts were hung up, colored with crayons, brown and black and bright red. When Thanksgiving was over, here came Santa Claus!

"I wish we could just keep Santa Claus in the windows the whole year around," Margie said.

Marly agreed. Besides vacation and presents and everything, it was as if she had three Christmas trees because she helped with three—their own, the school tree, and the Chris's tree. Mother sent for their old decorations, and it was fun to unpack them. Besides all the baubles and tinsel, there were special decorations to make. One simply went outside and picked sycamore balls and picked up pine cones of every size and then came in and gilded them and hung them on the tree with Christmas string.

Mother said shopping had never been so wonderful, because she simply went into town and took what was there without searching through store after store. She went with Mrs. Chris all one day, and Marly heard her say to Daddy when she came home after supper, "No crowded elevators! No artificial bells! No organs thundering *Silent Night* out over the busses and streetcars!"

Daddy laughed. "Lee, you were the city girl," he said.

Mother ran to him and sat on his lap and laughed. Marly felt so happy that it was almost as if it was Christmas already. She knew there wasn't any danger, this year, that Daddy wouldn't light the Christmas tree.

"Where's Joe?" Mother asked. "He can help me get the things out of the car if he won't pinch all the packages."

But Joe wasn't around. He wasn't in the house or in the barn or in the chicken coop or anywhere. Daddy remembered hearing him get his boots out after supper. Mother said, "Why didn't you ask him where he was going? It's starting to snow again."

"At Christmas time," Daddy said, "people are entitled to their secrets. For at least two weeks before Christmas, nobody should ever ask anybody where he is going."

That was true. But when it got very dark and snowed faster and faster and faster, Mother kept looking out of the window toward the road. "Did he take a flashlight?" she asked. "He shouldn't go off in weather like this. You never know. Do you suppose he was at Chris's when I came by and I didn't see him?"

She telephoned. But Joe wasn't there. Nobody had seen him at all.

It got later and later and later, and Marly was supposed to go to bed but nobody mentioned it. Daddy said, "Marly, doesn't he go with Margie's brothers sometimes? Could he be there?"

So she telephoned Margie's. But Joe hadn't been there at all.

"I'd better go out and look around again," Daddy said.

"Where will you look? Up and down the road?" Mother asked.

"Whatever possessed him to do such a thing without saying a word?" Daddy asked. "In winter, up here, people just don't wander around; he knows that." His voice sounded cross as he put on his gloves and boots and wound a scarf around his neck.

"Especially when it's started to snow," Mother said. She leaned toward the window, but there was no use because it was pitch-dark outside. Flakes pricked at the panes and made little whispers together.

Marly felt her heart beating hard when she looked out, pressing her face against the cold pane. Joe knows his way on all those roads, she thought, but they looked different all covered with snow. Sometimes the snow got so deep here, Mr. Chris said, that the fences disappeared entirely, and there weren't any roads at all. The pane misted over, and she couldn't see anything but herself reflected as if she sat outside in a little snowy room.

"Dale, it's after nine already," Mother said.

"I thought Joe knew better. Why, I never dreamed—I thought he'd just be going out for a minute, maybe to see about the goats or something." Daddy acted as if Mother blamed him for something he'd done and hadn't meant to do. "I'll fix Joe good for doing a thing like this," he said.

For days and days it had seemed as if Christmas was in the house already—all the good happy feelings, warmth and good smells, and the shining tree. Now all the goodness was suddenly gone from everything.

"It's good we've got the chains on," Daddy said. "I'll go by Chris's first, and on the way I'll honk, see, and if Joe hears me, he'll answer. Maybe he got off the road or something."

He was at the car, starting it, when the telephone rang. Mother ran to answer, saying on the way, "Marly, tell Daddy to wait a minute—"

Marly ran for the car without waiting for boots or anything, and Daddy waited and then sat still with the engine running and the lights shining through the white moving air. Mother was on the porch already, calling, as Marly ran back again.

"Dale, it was Chris. He and Fritz are getting the truck out. They'll be by for you. They don't think the car could make it anywhere tonight."

So Daddy came in again, standing near the door as he waited with his boots making puddles under him.

"Daddy, can't I go?" Marly asked. "Mother—"

"No!" It came from both of them at the same second, so she knew there wasn't a bit of use to ask again. "Why, look at your shoes; they're wet as sop," Mother said. "Marly, take those wet shoes off this instant."

At times like this a person obeyed everything in a hurry. Marly knew that. The truck came while she took off her shoes and socks, and she ran to the window to watch Daddy go out and the truck turn around and go away. They could hear it honking every little while as it went down the hill. Then they couldn't hear a thing except the flakes on the windows.

Mother said suddenly, "I'll make hot cocoa. Joe'll be cold when he gets back, and he loves hot cocoa. Marly, get your slippers on."

Thank goodness, she didn't say "Go to bed." Instead she made the best cocoa Marly ever tasted. She even went out to the car and brought in a package of marshmallows she'd meant to roll in nuts and chocolate for Christmas candy. Marly had a huge cup of cocoa with two fat marshmallows melting away on top. Mother even made toast and cut the pieces into little triangles and put on lots of butter. Enough for Joe and Daddy and Chris and Fritz. She kept making more and more, as if the longer they were gone the hungrier they were sure to be.

"It's simply silly to keep looking out of the windows," Mother said. "Shall we read something?" But she looked out of the window once more. "Why on earth Joe would do such a thing! Marly, isn't there *somewhere* you can think of—"

Then suddenly, thinking of Joe out in the cold while she sat in her warm robe and slippers drinking from her big foamy cup, Marly *knew*. It was the strangest thing. Suddenly she simply knew what Joe had done. That morning as they walked down to the road together on the way to the school bus stop, Joe had said something. "The only one not having any Christmas around here is Harry," he had said. "I'm going up and see him . . ."

Why on earth hadn't she remembered before?

"Mother, I think maybe he went to Harry's," she said.

"To Harry's? Marly, why on earth would he go to Harry's on a night like this?"

Marly told her what Joe had said. He had been so busy with school and Christmas coming and all that he hadn't been thinking about Harry lately at all. But at school one of his teachers had said, "Christmas is the time to think about people who are lonely. For somebody living all alone, Christmas can be the saddest time of the year."

"Well, then, of course that's where he went," Mother said.

She looked relieved, even though she went to look out of the window again. Now she was watching for the truck to come back. "It's probably nice and warm in Harry's little house," she said. "But why didn't Joe come back before it got dark? With it snowing so. He might have known how we'd worry."

"There must be a reason," Marly said, and stirred the island of marshmallow around and around in her cup.

"Here they come now!" Mother said from the window.

The truck came struggling and roaring up the hill. Before it stopped outside, Mother was on the porch, calling. "Is Joe with you?"

He was not. They came stamping in, and Mother let them talk and tell what they'd done already. They had gone up and down all the roads in every direction. There wasn't any use going any farther than Joe could possibly have walked. They had asked at every farm.

Then Mother asked, "Did you think of going to Harry's?"

"Why, no," Mr. Chris said, looking surprised. "Joe knows Harry's not there now, doesn't he? About now, when winter sets in good, he always goes to the Old Folks Home out by Erie. Chadwick, up his road, always keeps his goats till spring. Harry drove his goats over there a day or so ago."

"Did you even go by there, then?" Mother asked. And she told them what Joe had said.

So out to the truck again they went. They looked relieved and sounded relieved, too. Mr. Chris said Harry never seemed to lock his house, and Joe could have gone in and built a fire. That old lamp of Harry's couldn't even be seen from the road on a night like this. The roar of the truck drowned his voice before he finished, and the truck was gone again through the falling snow.

I hope it's so, I hope he's there. Please, please help Joe to be at Harry's house . . . Marly whispered to herself, not loud enough for Mother to hear. But Mother seemed to be whispering to herself, too. Everything was still except the fire cracking once in a while and that whispering of snow on the windowpanes.

After a while Mother said, "I keep wondering why he didn't come right back when he found Harry wasn't there. Why shouldn't he try coming back? But if he'd been on the road, on his way, surely they'd have found him . . ."

The worry settled over again like a fog.

The clock moved, but never in Marly's remembrance had it moved so slowly. Nine-thirty, nine thirty-five, nine-forty, a quarter to ten, and at last it struck ten. By then Mother was sitting on the very edge of her chair. And before the clock had finished striking, the telephone rang.

Mother leaped up and ran. Instead of saying "Hello" she said, "Yes? Yes?"

It was Daddy. Marly could hear the sound of his voice. She heard him say "All right" several times. She felt herself begin to breathe and knew she had been holding her breath deep down inside while she waited.

"Thank goodness!" Mother said. "But where are you?"

Marly couldn't hear what he answered. She thought they would talk forever. Mother saying, "Well, for goodness' sakes . . . Imagine that . . . How awful, Dale! Yes—yes, I see. Yes, I suppose you'd better . . ."

Marly felt as if she would burst out of her skin. She began to jerk at Mother's arm. "Mother, where is he? Did he find Joe? Did he?"

"Hush, Marly . . . Yes, yes, they found Joe all right . . ." And into the telephone again, "What a relief! An hour? Well, then, I'll get Marly to bed."

And she hung up at last.

"Mother, what did he say?" Marly cried. And Mother leaned down and took her close and hugged her and began to laugh.

"Marly, Joe has done the most wonderful thing," she said. "You were right about where he went. He was meaning to come right back, he said, but when he got to Harry's, nobody was there. But the back door was standing open. He went in but nobody was there, and he called but Harry didn't answer. And then he went out back of the place where the path goes down to the spring and . . ." Mother reached up and wiped her eyes.

"I know where," Marly said.

"It seems that Harry had gone to get his cheeses up to the house before he left and had slipped on the ice and hurt his leg. Chris says if Joe hadn't happened to go there today, he'd have frozen. Imagine . . ." Her eyes were full of tears again, but she just let them go on running this time. "Marly, Joe got that old man up the steps and into his bed and built a fire and gave him hot milk!" she said.

Marly lay awake in bed, imagining how it had been. Why couldn't she have gone with Joe this time? She could have helped with everything. She could have helped with the fire and heated the milk while Joe got Harry into bed. Then Mother would have said, "Marly and Joe have done something wonderful . . ."

But she was only a little bit jealous about Joe being such a hero. She was mostly proud enough to die. When she heard the truck come back and Joe and Daddy came in, she couldn't bear just lying still, so she rushed downstairs. They didn't scold her at all but let her sit by the fire while Joe told it all over again. He sipped at his cocoa and talked and talked. He acted quite smart about it, but then, who wouldn't?

Harry was at Chris's house now, in with Fritz, where there was a couch and a nice stove.

At last they all went upstairs together. Joe stood by his door as if he rather hated it all to end, as tired as he was—the way a person will stand Christmas night or at the end of the Fourth of July when the last of the fireworks is over.

"Joe, what a *Christmas*-thing to do!" Marly said.

It was queer, though, what happened the very next morning. As Marly came downstairs, she heard Mother say, "Oh, *no*, Joe! He's such a dirty old man! That awful smell—"

"I don't care. He can have my room. I'll sleep on the couch," Joe said.

"Joe, surely there's somewhere else he can go—where his leg can be taken care of."

"I want him here," Joe said.

Mother looked at Daddy. Daddy opened the stove door and shoved in some coal, hard. "It's Christmas, Lee," he said. "If Joe thinks that's what people should do at Christmas, I guess maybe he's right."

"I'll wait on him. You won't have to do a thing," Joe said. "I can carry his meals up, and he can come down and see the tree and everything a little while. We can help him up and down, Marly and me."

"*Honestly!*" Mother said in a helpless way. "Dale, he must have bedbugs and everything, living the way he does."

Daddy stood there looking at her. His eyes looked hot in his face, which seemed to be going pale. The air had a big important feeling all around him, the way it has around an actor with all the lights turned on him alone, with everybody waiting to hear him speak. "Lee, we had bugs in that prison camp," Daddy said. "I had them on me when I came out. But we got rid of them before we got home again. Some of the people in camp helped each other all the time. Some others never thought about anything or anybody but themselves. I'd never known before how different people can be. And now Joe—" He turned and looked at Joe with the proudest look Marly ever saw in her life. "Well, I know now that Joe would have been one of the good ones. I just know that now."

Marly had never seen Mother look so crushed and so hurt. Even when Daddy had been cross and tired all that time. Even when he first came home and was so thin and sad.

"Well, of course Harry must come here, then," Mother said. Her voice was slow but very firm. "I'll go and call Chrissie and tell her so." She went to the telephone and rang the little bell and waited, looking at the floor and listening. Daddy stood where he was, and Joe sat looking at the eggs on his plate. The kitchen was very still. Outside the sun was shining on bright new snow.

It was like last night again, hearing only Mother's end of the conversation. "Chrissie, Joe wants Harry here for Christmas. Please tell him. Yes, Joe insists—and tell him we all want him to come. All of us. Yes. I do, too. Yes—please tell him."

She hung up.

Daddy went over and kissed her square on the mouth. "Merry Christmas, Lee," he said.

Marly felt herself light and strong and happy. It was as if today, which was nothing but the Friday before Christmas, had gone running ahead over the calendar, and it was already Christmas Day.

11 THE BEGINNING AGAIN

Mr. Chris said the time between Christmas and spring was always the longest time of the year. It's true, Marly thought, going to school day after day. Snow fell and fell and melted and melted and then fell again. The roads were icy and piled on either side with old drifts as high as the car. Harry had gone again after Christmas, and the new gifts got to be just ordinary things lying around with the things you'd had forever and forever.

Valentine's Day was fun at school, of course, and the windows looked bright with red and white hearts and streamers. Then came the heaviest snow of all, a storm Mr. Chris said was one of the worst in history. The school bus didn't come for four solid days. Wind howled around the house the way it did on the radio for a ghost story, and Marly shivered in bed and covered herself clear to the eyes.

A week after Valentine's Day the sun came out suddenly. The world was a blaze of light, and the snow began to sink into the ground. The tops of the fences appeared again, and Joe measured how much more of the posts he could see every day. The ground appeared, brown, on the south side of the hill. Trees stood bare again, with patches of white snow still lying where their shadows fell.

Then the miracle happened.

One day Marly was on the way home from school and saw Mother coming to meet her down the road. Mother waved and shouted long before Marly could understand what she was saying. But then she heard it:

"Marly, Mr. Chris said to tell you. The sap's up! It's sugaring time again!"

The sap's up!

Sugaring time!

"When do we go over? Now?" Marly cried.

"Fritz came for Daddy, and I'm to bring you and Joe. They need help, hanging buckets." Mother looked all excited herself, her cheeks bright red. "Put on your oldest things—" Marly was already on her way. "And don't forget your boots—and your mittens. Those buckets will be cold."

How familiar the hill was now! Marly knew it as they went in the little old road, every rut of it practically, as she might know the face of an old friend. One year ago she had come along there alone, wondering about everything, and there—there by the woodpile—she had found Mr. Chris. Now a high new pile of wood stood ready, almost as high as the little brown house.

There was no fire yet, this time. The evaporator was being assembled. Long scrubbed pans had been lifted over the firebox. Marly could see the section where the sap would be, first as thin as water, then flowing into the next pan, darker, and the next, darker still. Darker and darker until it was not sap any more at all. But syrup. Real honest-to-goodness first-run Chris. She was so excited her hands got trembly, and she didn't know whether she was going to be a bit of use. Daddy was piling buckets onto the truck from

143

the lean-to where they'd been stored, upside down, all winter.

It was like seeing the beginning of everything. The very, *very* beginning. Her eyes moved out over the sugarbush; patches of snow and deep brown leaves lay on the ground under the bare trees. Surprises were good, she thought. But a miracle was better when you knew it was coming. This year she knew. She knew exactly where the spring beauties would appear. She knew where hepaticas would turn the ground blue and lavender and pink. She knew where trillium would stand tall, its leaves saying "three" and its petals saying "three." She knew where the bloodroot would light its white Easter candles.

So many things to begin again! She knew how the leaves would come green on the trees, how their flowers would turn the soft maples red along the brook. She knew where water would go tumbling as the snow melted, making waterfalls that were there only in the spring. She lifted her face to the sun and laughed. Spring sparkled already in the sharp air.

There was a sudden whirring among the trees. What was that? Had a sudden army of cicadas arrived already? Mr. Chris was laughing and calling her to come along smart with those buckets. She could hear his voice a long way up the hill.

The whirring came from what Fritz was doing. He had a thing he called a brace and bit, and he and Mr. Chris were going from tree to tree, drilling holes with it. They hammered sharp little drippers they called *spiles* into the holes. Over each of these on a special little hook at the top, Joe and Marly were to hang a bucket and put on each one its little pointed hat of a lid.

Every hole must be in a new and different place from those of last year and the years before. The old ones had grown over like scars on a vaccination. Marly could find on each tree, especially on the biggest ones, where holes had been made for years and years. But Mr. Chris said this never seemed to harm a tree at all. "No more than those little scars you've got from tumbling around when you were little," he said.

The sap was coming so fast that before they got the buckets on the spiles were dripping. At once, into the empty tin pails, the sap began to go plop! plop! plop!

"They'll be full by morning at this rate," Fritz said. "Chris, you don't think it'll freeze?"

"No, this is a prize first run. I can smell it!"

It was fun to walk along behind them and listen to the sugar-talk.

"It's wonderful, an early run like this. It has to be about 40° to bring it up. There've been years when we didn't even open the bush, but not this year, thank goodness, the way we need the cash . . . I've known it to stay on cold and stay on cold until it was time to plant the oats." Mr. Chris's voice boomed out among the trees as he talked to Daddy and Mother. "After we start planting, there's no time for sugaring. You plant oats early and you get oats; you plant 'em late and you get nothing but chaff."

This was the way Marly liked Mr. Chris best. Unless it was when he put wood on the fire and sat down and talked while it burned, and the steam began rising in white clouds once more under the little roof. Unless it was when he got that watchful look on his face as he lifted syrup from the last pan into his wooden paddle—and let—it—slowly—drip—

145

to—see—whether—it—was—thick—enough. When he did that, Marly knew she would hold her breath.

Plop! plop! went the sap behind her as she hung one bucket after another. Her hands were cold soon, but she didn't care.

"First time I made sugar in this bush, my father had nothing but one iron kettle. Not much better than the Indians; they're the ones that taught my grandfather, Dale, on this same land. Later we had a half dozen kettles set in a row, with a fire under each. We poured from kettle to kettle as it boiled down—and did we have to hurry with the sugaring-off kettle before it burned! It was set on a sweep-pole we could swing off the fire in a hurry."

"Maybe that's the way I'd better start, on Maple Hill," Daddy said. "Nothing like starting at the beginning."

"No, no, we'll go on over and do your trees as soon as we're through here. We can do it all together and keep track, can't we? You can haul your sap over every time you're filled up."

Joe said, "Maybe we'd better build our own place and do it the old way, Mr. Chris. Harry says syrup's not as good as it used to be when it got all full of twigs and bark and stuff."

"And spiders," said Mr. Chris. "Oh, yes, Harry's right— we're altogether too fussy now. We strain it when we gather and strain it when it goes into the evaporator, and then we filter it again when it comes off the fire."

Dark came too soon. Only five hundred buckets were hung. But thank goodness, Marly thought, tomorrow was Saturday. They could work all day long in the bright sunny air. From the red sunset, Mr. Chris said, you could tell what a good day it was going to be tomorrow.

Going back to the house, walking slowly, Mr. Chris said, "Marly, my Dad used to say me a poem every sugaring time. He said it was so I'd not overdo the tasting part of it. Maybe I'd better give it to you and Joe. It went like this:

> *My boyish enjoyment was complete*
> *And once a year my face was sweet!*
> *But woe to him who takes no care,*
> *And lets his taste become his snare!*
> *'Twere well if Eve had tasted less.*
> *And so with me, I must confess.*
> *Eve, I suppose, grew sick at heart,*
> *But I ached in another part!"*

Maybe it was good advice. But Marly knew she could hardly wait for the first taste.

Mother called her early the next morning, so early her room was still dark. She was so sleepy she had to fight to unravel her clothes and find where her feet and arms went. But up the stairs came the smell of bacon frying already, and when she almost fell downstairs, the kitchen was bright and full of laughter. Fritz had come already to help tap their trees.

"Sleepyhead!" Joe yelled, and came after her with a cold washcloth. This time she didn't even care, though she squealed and squealed. She felt herself come alive as he splashed cold water over her face.

Outside was the smell of spring.

"We've got an east wind today," Fritz said, sniffing. At his heels, the dog Tony was sniffing the same way. "A north wind will stop a run. And Chris says a south wind blows the sap right back up the spiles."

When they finally got back to Mr. Chris's bush, Marly could hardly wait to see what was in the buckets. She took off the first pointed lid she came to. The bucket was almost full. The sap was as bright and clear as spring water. It didn't taste very sweet when she put a finger in and tasted—only faintly sweet, like something far off that you barely heard, or barely saw. There was no color in it at all—or was there? Just a touch of yellow, maybe, in its brightness? She peered in and thought she must see it, for she knew it was surely there.

In an hour the woods were full of steam again. The smell of woodsmoke drifted down the hill and among the trees. Then came the first smell of sweetness . . . Was it?

It's the beginning, Marly thought. Just as Mr. Chris had said, the syrup is spring. It's the heart and blood of the maple trees; it has the gold of the leaves in it and the brown of the bark. It's the sun shining. It's snow melting. It's the bright new air and the earth as it starts pushing— pushing—pushing.

Her arms felt strong. Her heart was light.

"We'll be boiling late tonight," Mr. Chris said.

"We'll come over the way we did last year," Daddy answered. "This time we may be of a little use." From Daddy's voice, the way he said the words, Marly knew he felt all the bright new feelings she felt herself. From Joe's face, she knew he felt it, too.

On such a day, it is hard to believe how quickly every feeling, every goodness, can change and go away. None of them knew how quickly as they sat around again that night, as Daddy sang once more about the foxes, as the fire burned and the miracle of the cream happened all over again. This time Mr. Chris let her make the miracle happen herself, and she felt like a fairy queen with a wand as she made the high bubbles fall back and behave themselves.

But before dawn the next morning, she woke with a start. Fritz was downstairs already. She could hear him talking to Daddy who was only halfway downstairs, still in his pajamas.

"Chrissie came and woke me. About two o'clock it was, I guess. He overdid yesterday—getting that first run out just right. I'll try to get back by afternoon if he's okay. If you can get help with the gathering—but of course it's Sunday . . ."

If he's okay? Who?

Marly felt her heart sink down. Fritz rushed outside, and she heard the car start with a roar. Joe was standing in the hall when she went out, and Mother, in her robe. Daddy said, "Lee, he said Chris woke with this numbness, and then when he tried to stand, he couldn't. They've got an ambulance coming. Chrissie called the doctor and he said—"

Marly sat down, right on the floor. Everything seemed to go dizzy and ugly and horrible. What was spring? What was anything?

12 NO MORE DRUMSTICKS?

"Do you think we can do it?" Daddy asked.

Mother looked as if she was surprised he could ask such a silly question. "People do what they have to do," she said. "Chris needs this crop, and he's going to get it. Fritz knows *how*. We just need to help him."

"Chris has always done the real job, the finishing," Daddy said.

"Well, now he's sick," Mother said. Her voice sounded impatient, but Marly knew it was because she was so worried. "He's going to need the money from the sugar crop more than ever. The sap's there, the wood's cut, and just look at the help!"

Marly lifted her chin and made her muscles go hard on her arms. Joe got his determined look; it made him look older, almost as if he was ready to be a man already. "Sure we can do it," he said.

"It'll be hard work," Daddy said in a warning voice. He looked at them, first at Marly and then at Joe. "If we start this thing, we finish it. See?"

Joe looked down at his plate and so did Marly. They didn't always like hard work, goodness knows, and sometimes they figured all kinds of ways to get out of it. But

that was dishes and wood-chopping and things like that—
not sugaring!

"We can do the way Fritz said and just finish off this
first run," Daddy said. "Or we can carry on just like Chris
has always done himself. He needs the money, the way
Mother says. It's some of the cash he depends on. Then—
well—" He looked at his plate, too. "It's something we can
do that'd make him feel good."

Nobody even thought about the next day being school
again.

First they gathered their own hill. There were not quite
fifty trees, but by the time each bucket had been tipped
off the spile with its lid taken off, the sap poured into a
gathering bucket, and the lid put back, Marly was already
feeling tired in her arms. Then they went to Mr. Chris's
huge bush. Marly didn't know how huge it was. Those
trees with their full buckets went marching on and on and
on. Daddy drove the horses to pull the flatboat with its
huge tank because it was too steep and muddy for the
tractor in this bush. Marly had never even known there
was *another* sugarbush besides the one Fritz had tapped,
over the fields beyond Chris's place at the edge of the
deep woods. In all there were over fourteen hundred
buckets.

Soon her hands were numb. At first she wore gloves, but
the sap splashed, and they got wet and cold, so she took
them off. At first, too, she hated to splash a single drop
of the precious stuff. But soon she knew it didn't matter
much if some splashed out. She was wet all down her
front, absolutely sopping with spring, as Mother said.
But Mother was sopping with spring, too, and Daddy, and
Joe. Mother got so tired she offered to watch the fire for

a while. At first it was Daddy who kept going back to keep it burning.

Goodness, but it was a relief to see Fritz coming at last.

"How is he?" Mother asked. Marly wanted to ask, but she couldn't for the big lump that settled square in the middle of her throat at the very idea of Mr. Chris being sick at all.

You could tell from Fritz's face before he answered that he felt sad, and Marly felt everything inside of herself turning heavy and cold.

"He's coming along, I guess. Anyway, he's still *here*," Fritz said. He used the words people use all the time; he said Mr. Chris was "as well as could be expected."

At the word "here," Marly hurried back into the trees. It didn't mean that Mr. Chris was here in the sugarbush under the blue sky where he belonged. It only meant he was still in the world. But for now it had to be enough.

They all went back to work. By two o'clock the gathering was finished. Fritz insisted they go home for a while, and he would watch the fire at the sugar camp. But Daddy said, "No, I'd rather stay." He could sleep here this time, he said. Fritz had to have some rest before he'd be worth a grain of salt tomorrow. The sap was still coming. Slowly, steadily, the buckets were filling up again.

Marly had never been more glad to get her supper, never more glad for a warm bath and her warm bed. She scarcely remembered when she fell onto the pillow. Suddenly Mother was waking her up again, and it was morning.

"Time to go," Mother said.

Marly's overalls were stiff down the front, but they were dry at least. The bacon smelled wonderful. She stumbled toward the smell and the warm kitchen. Fritz was already eating; he was going to fetch Daddy, and then they'd all go out again.

"This reminds me of stories I've heard about the old days," Fritz said. "Folks used to help each other more than they do now. If a man's barn burned in my neighborhood, why, everybody turned to and in a week he had another barn—full of hay."

"That's the way it should be," Mother said.

Marly wanted terribly to ask for news of Mr. Chris. But it was like yesterday; she couldn't get the words out of her throat. She knew that Chrissie would come back when there was no more danger, and not until. So that meant, as long as Fritz was eating *here*—

Just before he left, though, she had to ask. "Fritz, have you heard—? Did Chrissie call or anything?" She saw how Joe looked up, listening. The room got still because Mother had even stopped washing the dishes to listen.

"Ya. She called," Fritz said. "He's some better than yesterday, they think. But it'll be a day or so before they can really tell for sure." He looked down as he spoke, and the cap in his hand turned around and around. "You know, the thing folks always said about Chris was how big-hearted he was—always thinking about other folks. And now—well, his heart really *is* big, see. Sort of swollen or something—"

He turned quickly and went out. Nobody spoke. Mother began scraping mush from the bottom of the kettle, and the scraping sounded loud in the room. Marly suddenly couldn't keep it back any more. She leaned forward against the table and began to cry. Not loud, just steady, steady, steady, like the sap into the buckets.

"That's not going to help any," Joe said, suddenly as

angry as he could be. "If that isn't just like a girl!"

She looked up and saw him glaring at her. "You don't even *care!*" she cried. "You're the *meanest—*"

Mother said, "Now, now—"

But Joe leaned across the table toward Marly as if he wanted to scorch her to a crisp with his eyes. "I'm not going to waste my time crying," he said. "I'm working for Mr. Chris. See? We've got things to do, and there's no use thinking about anything but getting them done. Dad and I talked about it last night. He said there's no use worrying. Is worry going to help Mr. Chris any? All we've got to do is *work.*"

It was true. She sat up straight again and reached down into her pockets to find her handkerchief. After a minute she began to eat.

Then Daddy came. He told them how it had been to stay at the camp all night. He'd got to know some of Chris's mice, he said. "And just after dawn, guess who paid me a visit? *Four* deer. They practically knocked on the door." He looked tired, but he didn't look tired in the same way he used to look tired. Not at all. It was a *kind* tiredness, all soft instead of sharp and mean.

So another long day began. They had been working on the hill for two hours already when they saw the bright yellow school bus go by on the road.

"Joe, it's school today!" Marly said.

He laughed. "Not for us, it isn't," he said.

The flatboat dragged along the little deep-rutted roads that wound through the bush. Marly knew their pattern now. Over the years the roads had been worked out so the gathering was as easy as possible. Fritz would drive along and stop, and then he and she and Joe took their big buckets and separated, each having certain trees. She could carry three small bucketsful in her bucket, but it was so heavy she couldn't lift it to dump it into the high tank on the flatboat. Each time she had to wait for Fritz or Joe to come and empty it. But she got so she could fill her bucket as fast as they did and get it back with them almost every time so they didn't have to wait for her. One arm got so tired she had to carry with the other; she got so she could even switch the full bucket from side to side without spilling much. She got handy with the little lids, too, so she could slide one off and put it under her left arm while she dumped the sap into her bucket. Then she could slip it back on with one hand without having to set her bucket down. There was a right way to do everything. Her arms were lame from the day before, but after a while she forgot to notice. It was as if her tiredness put her arms to sleep. Yet she worked. She stayed right along with Joe until the last bucket was emptied and Fritz called, "That's the last one!"

She had never heard more beautiful words in all her life. Never, either, had the sugar camp looked so good. She went in and sank down on the old couch, and Daddy smiled at her.

"Good work," he said. "Fritz says you're the eighth wonder of the world."

She was too tired to be very pleased, even. She was limp inside and outside. But after a while Fritz brought some eggs and boiled them in the syrup. They tasted wonderful, with some of the sweetness in them as if it had gone right through the shells. Mother came with sandwiches and hot coffee and cold milk. As wonderful as that little brown house had been before, it had never seemed as wonderful as now. Just to sit down was wonderful. To eat was a joy. Even to feel the wet cold of her overalls drying by the fire was a goodness. This was why Mr. Chris loved sugaring time. Now she knew it. He loved not only spring coming and the warm fire and the good tastes and lovely smells, but cutting wood and hanging buckets and gathering sap and watching the slow change from plain watery sap to the deep amber of the finished syrup. And he loved the work itself.

After she ate, she almost felt as if she could start all over and not mind at all.

But to think about Mr. Chris made all the goodness in her change and seem to go thick, like milk curdling on a hot day. It was as it had been in the morning. When Fritz went to the house and came back again, she was afraid to ask him what he had found out.

He told them, as before, without being asked. The same old empty words—"as well as can be expected."

So another day ended. With evening it was colder, and Fritz looked at the sky and said, "I hope it doesn't freeze. If it froze tonight with all that sap in the buckets, we'd lose every bucket on the whole place."

"What do you mean—lose every bucket?" Joe asked.

"You're the scientist around here, Joe," Fritz said. "What happens when water freezes? Swells, doesn't it? Well, if sap freezes in full buckets, sometimes all the seams split, and there we are. A leaky bucket's no good for man or beast."

"Sure it isn't," Joe said. Then he added quickly, "That means we've got to keep 'em emptied, doesn't it?"

"That's just it." Fritz sighed, and Marly understood why.

The idea of starting a whole new gathering made her ache from her head to her toes.

"There's just no breathing spell while the run's on," Fritz said. "There's so much to be careful about in this business. Outside, we have to see that the buckets don't burst. In here, if the syrup boils down too far, you can burn out a pan and cost yourself a few hundred dollars in ten minutes. It's not only a batch of sap you lose but the whole thing."

They were all very still for a while. Then Daddy said, "Fritz, I just drew some more syrup off. I'd like you to look at it."

Marly held her breath while Fritz looked and tasted. Daddy had finished off gallons and gallons now, but he was anxious over every one.

"I was thinking, Fritz," he said, "we can keep this syrup in another place from the batch Chris finished before he left. See? Maybe it's not as good. How could it be? So I thought maybe he wouldn't want his good old customers to get some of ours. He told me about all the folks that have bought his syrup year after year."

Fritz stood tasting from the cup. "It tastes mighty good to me, Dale," he said, and smacked his lips.

It tasted mighty good to Marly, too. Mother took some of it home and actually fried pancakes for supper. You wouldn't have thought anybody'd want syrup for supper, but everybody did. Daddy said, "Well—our syrup!" He and Joe ate stacks of pancakes big enough, as Mother said, to sink a ship.

After Daddy went back to the sugar camp, Marly expected she'd fall asleep the way she had the night before. But she didn't. She was all clean and warm and tired, yet she couldn't go to sleep at all.

She just kept thinking about Mr. Chris. If there was only something she could do besides work and say her prayers! But there wasn't anything—not anything at all. She had written a note for Fritz to take, but it had been hard to think of anything to say, and she knew it wasn't really anything Mr. Chris wouldn't know already. As she lay in bed, she kept thinking about Mr. Chris lying still in a high white bed, up in the hospital. She had never seen him lying down, and the idea of him lying sick was like a wave of blackness over her mind. It was like thinking of bloodroot and witches, or of mushrooms called "destroying angels" and "death cups." In the woods there were so many old dead things—all those logs covered with fungus, and horrible little bugs running under stones, and worms spoiling the maple leaves so sometimes the sound of their chewing sounded like rain.

She lay with her eyes closed tight, so tight the lids began to ache. But poison things and ugly things and cruel things kept crawling through her mind. She even began to feel, after a while, as if there was something crawling over her skin. She turned on the light once to see, searching through the sheets. But no! Of course there wasn't a bug anywhere.

When she lay down again, she left the light burning. But it didn't take the ugly thoughts away. Mr. Chris himself had said there had to be lots of dead things so there could be lots of living things. It was awful to think about. The little foxes eating the nice little chickens and baby mice. She and Joe had found neat little bones by the doors of the den and tufts of fur and feathers. Even her nice cat was always eating birds unless she watched him. Once he ate a cardinal right on the kitchen step.

Laughing, Mr. Chris had said once, "Now, Marly—I

guess you're not going to eat any more drumsticks or any more eggs? No more pork chops?"

They had all laughed about it then. She could hear them laughing, in her mind. It was the way, of course—everything eating something; everybody eating somebody. Even Mr. Chris and Daddy and Mother and Joe and herself— they were always eating drumsticks, every single one of them. But there was a reason for it, as Mr. Chris said; it was to stay alive.

But about Mr. Chris being sick, there wasn't any reason in the whole world that she could think of. Mr. Chris not to be alive any more? There couldn't be any reason for that. So big and strong, as alive as a tree. Doing good in every direction, all the time.

But she kept thinking about that one big maple tree he had cut down because it was, as he said, "dying from the heart."

She tried to think of every pleasant and beautiful and wonderful thing she knew. She made a list of all the miracles in her mind. She recited poems to herself and sang softly all the songs she'd learned at school and all the songs Daddy sang. But it wasn't any good. Finally she couldn't bear it any longer and got up and crept softly down the stairs. She sat on a chair by the stove, her feet gathered under her. But it was cold in the kitchen, and she had to stir the fire up and put in some wood and coal. As quiet as she tried to be, Mother heard her. She heard Mother getting up and then the sound of footsteps down the stairs.

"Mother, I didn't mean to wake you up . . ."

"It's all right. I wasn't sleeping very well myself," Mother said. "I guess we're just too tired, that's all."

"I keep thinking about Mr. Chris," Marly said.

Thank goodness Joe hadn't come down, so she could cry all she needed to. Mother didn't say a word but only heated some milk, and they sat with their feet on the oven door and sipped at their steaming cups. Marly was glad for the silence and the warmth; it was cozy to sit with Mother in the night with the clock ticking and ticking and the fire crackling and the kettle slowly steaming.

At last Mother put down her empty cup and said, "Come back to bed with me this time." So they went up the stairs together.

This time Marly didn't even know when she went to sleep. When she woke up, the sun was shining and Joe had already gone off with Fritz. "Shall we hurry?" Mother asked. When they started out, she said, "Thank goodness it didn't freeze. We're all right for another day."

The sap was still coming and coming and coming, as if the earth could never give enough. How could they go on and on and on? Daddy looked quite gray. Fritz was red-faced and didn't say anything most of the morning. By noon both Marly and Joe were almost too tired to talk.

"I don't know . . . If I could find some help, maybe we could do it," Fritz said. "But I've called everybody. Everybody's having his own big run, same as we are."

"I understand now why Chrissie said she hated sugar season," Mother said.

Daddy had brought his little radio to the sugarhouse to keep him awake in the night and to keep him company. "Said in the news this morning it was apt to be the best sugar year in New England history," he said. Marly couldn't tell whether his voice was glad or not. He was just trying to make it sound glad.

Then Fritz went to the house as he did every day. When they saw him coming back, they were already gathering in the second bush. Joe was driving the horses and saying "Gee" and "Haw" and everything. When he saw Fritz coming, he said suddenly "Whoa!" and they all waited. But even at a distance they could tell that something was different. Fritz started shouting halfway up the hill.

"He's a lot better today!" he cried. He was panting and smiling. "Chrissie said she might even come home for a while tonight. I'm driving in after her when we've got through this bush . . ."

That afternoon Marly had to add another miracle to the list. It was how light a heavy bucket could suddenly be.

That night she slept.

13 ANNIE-GET-YOUR-GUN

The next morning a visitor came up onto the hill. Marly saw her coming. She looked familiar some way, a solid sort of woman, with a very settled-looking hat and her neck all wrapped in a big woolly scarf. She picked her way carefully along the deep muddy ruts and looked as cross as an old patch.

"Who on earth is that?" Mother asked.

Joe shaded his eyes. "Golly!" he said. "She's the nurse from school. Miss Annie. She helped with the vaccinations."

Mother stood still, watching Miss Annie coming, and then she put her bucket down and went to meet her. Marly could hear their voices but not what they were saying. Miss Annie's voice sounded like a teacher's on a day when everybody didn't behave.

Mother turned and called, "Marly! Joe!" She looked terribly upset.

"This is Miss Annie Nelson," she said. "She says she's the county truant officer."

Oh, my goodness! The truant officer!

"I came to see whether you were sick, you two," Miss Annie said, looking them up and looking them down with

164

her sharp eyes. "But you're about the two healthiest-looking specimens I've seen in a long time."

"I've told her what you're doing," Mother said, her forehead going wrinkly with concern, "but it seems that there aren't . . . Well, there seem to be *rules—*"

Miss Annie was looking at Joe. "Have they told you what they call me downtown at the school?" she asked. Her eyes were glittery sharp, but her mouth looked as if it might laugh, Marly thought, if she'd only let it.

"No. I never heard," Joe said uncomfortably.

"Well, they call me Annie-Get-Your-Gun!" she said. "Nobody gets away with playing hooky from *my* schools."

"I'm sure Joe wouldn't want to," Mother said. "It's only that we—" Her eyes swept over the sugarbush.

"Well, one thing I know is that I'm freezing stiff," Miss Annie said. "Maybe we could go in that place where the fire is and talk this business over."

"Yes, yes, of course," Mother said. "And my husband—we can talk to my husband about it. I taught school myself for a while before I married, and of course I know how it is. You simply can't let children stay out for any little reason."

"No, you can't," said Annie-Get-Your-Gun.

Daddy was putting some more logs on the fire when they went in. Miss Annie stood inside the door, watching him.

"This is my husband," Mother said.

But Annie paid no attention. She stood looking around while she began to unwind her scarf. "Well, well, I declare!" she said. "I've lived around this part of the country all my life, and I've never actually been inside one of these places. Of course I see plenty of them from the road,

all that smoke and steam. Heard they were syrup places."

"Sugar camps," said Joe.

She looked at him. "I guess you know all about it, young man?" she asked sharply. Marly thought, Oh, dear, why did Joe have to go and act smarty just now, with a truant officer?

"Yes, ma'am, I guess I do," Joe said.

"Won't you sit down?" Daddy asked hurriedly.

But Miss Annie didn't sit down for a while. She walked around the evaporator, asking questions. She wanted to know how much sap it took to make a gallon of syrup. She wanted to know how much wood it took to keep the fire going. She wanted to know more things than you could shake a stick at, as Mr. Chris might have said. And talking about shaking a stick—when the bubbles started rising high, Daddy let Joe do the magic trick. Marly wanted to do it herself, but after all this was the truant officer from Joe's school, so she didn't say a single word.

"Well, think of that!" Miss Annie said. "Why, that's the most surprising thing I ever saw. I've never even thought about syrup. Why, I never . . ." She asked more and more questions.

Then, finally, Daddy offered her a taste.

She stood with the steam coming out of the tin cup in her hand, sniffing at it as if she was a little bit suspicious. "Smells like sweet corn cooking, only better," she said. "It smells like—" She had a way of stopping her sentences in the middle.

"It smells like spring," Marly said, to help out.

Miss Annie gave her a quick look, surprised. "Yes. Yes, of course it does—like a spring morning." She took a deep breath over the cup. "After a rain, maybe," she said, and reached her tongue out, tasting the very edge. The cup was hot, and she pulled her tongue in again in a hurry.

"Let me set the cup in the snow a minute. There's still a drift back of the sugarhouse," Joe said.

When he brought the syrup back, just right to drink, Miss Annie was sitting by Daddy and Mother on the old couch. She was eating a boiled egg.

"I declare I never tasted anything so grand in my life," she said. "My grandfather used to say, I remember, that anything but first-run syrup was an insult to his appetite. I think people have forgotten how good these things can be."

"Especially things they make themselves," Mother said, smiling. "We came from the city a year ago, and we've said that over and over."

Suddenly Miss Annie seemed excited. She looked at Joe and then at Marly, and her eyes began to sparkle over her cup. "Children ought to learn about that," she said. "Why, every child ought to come out here and have a taste—" She stopped again. But Marly could see the thought finished on her face. "Every child in that school ought to see a place like this. It's part of their American heritage, that what it is, and they don't even know it."

"Sometimes teachers do bring their classes here. Mr. Chris told me," Marly said.

"Field trips," said Joe.

"Well, I'm glad to hear it." Miss Annie's eyes had a real sparkle now that she was warm and full of sap. "But how did this sugar-thing start? I mean who discovered you could get *that*—" she pointed to the deep amber of the last pan that was draining slowly out into the can, "—from *that?*" She pointed to the first long pan at the back, where pale watery sap was running in from the storage tank.

"Mr. Chris said it came right from the Indians," Marly said.

Miss Annie turned to her. "But how did *they* find it out?" she asked.

None of them knew exactly how that had happened. Even Fritz didn't know. When Miss Annie went off down the hill again, the last thing she said was, "I'm going to find out if *anybody* knows how those Indians knew!"

The next to last thing she said was to Mother. "Now, you just don't worry about school for a few days for that pair of yours. If they had the measles, they'd be excused, and they'd come back after and get along just fine. They're getting part of their education right here in this sugarbush, and I don't mind reporting what I think to the principal."

Mother watched her out of sight, and turned with a smile. "Well, I guess we converted *her*," she said.

"The syrup did it," Joe said.

But Marly was sure it had been the miracle. It was an odd thing, she thought, how one miracle seemed to make another. And later that evening, she really knew how true it was. They were finishing supper when the telephone rang. Marly answered. She loved to answer and always tried to beat Joe to it if she could. Sometimes they argued over the receiver, and Mother had to take it away from both of them before the person who was calling thought there was a house afire. Tonight, though, Joe was so tired he didn't even get up from his chair.

"Hello. This is Annie-Get-Your-Gun," came over the telephone.

169

"Who?" For a minute Marly was too surprised to re- member.

"This is Miss Annie, the lady who came to the sugar- bush today—the truant officer."

"Oh. Yes—"

"Well, I talked to the principal, and I talked to the su- perintendent. They both said to talk to Joe's teacher, so I did."

Goodness, Marly thought, all that fuss because Joe stayed out of school.

"The teacher talked to the class, and . . . Maybe I'd better speak to your father?"

"My daddy's not here. He's out at the sugar camp," Marly said.

Mother was listening. "I'll talk to her, Marly," she said.

"My mother is here—"

Miss Annie's voice was so sharp and loud that Marly could still hear every word she said, even after Mother took the receiver. Besides, Mother held it about five inches away, so Miss Annie's voice wouldn't hurt her ear. Miss Annie told about the principal and the superintendent all over again. Then she said, "Joe's teacher agreed with me that nothing on earth could do those kids more good than coming out there to help—if they *could* help and not be in the way. Or maybe just some of the strongest boys? Your husband said you needed help."

"Why, yes—we *do*—" Mother's eyes went wide.

"Well, then, how many do you want?" Miss Annie asked briskly. "If you'll find out from your husband, there's no reason why the bus couldn't bring all the boys you need right to the spot in the morning."

"Why, that's wonderful!" Mother said. "I'll go right on over and ask him and Fritz."

Miss Annie told her where to call back, and Mother wrote it down with her fingers trembling. She hung up before Miss Annie had entirely finished with her fourth good-by. Then she just stood there for a minute, looking amazed. "Well, imagine that," she said.

In an hour she called Miss Annie back again. If a dozen boys could come the first day, later they'd see what happened to the weather. It looked to Fritz as if it might freeze any day now, and keeping the sap gathered would be a wonderful help. Then there might be a rest for a while if the cold snap held. Then, of course, in another thaw, there'd be another run.

"We've decided the boys can take turns at it," Miss Annie said. "No one boy is going to suffer much loss of school if those runs last a solid month or more."

Marly stood by the telephone, poking Mother with her elbow. "Mother—ask her why the *girls* can't come. Why, I can carry as many buckets as Joe can!"

"You can't either!" said Joe.

"I can!"

"Ssssh!" Mother said.

There was a little silence on the other end of the phone. Then Miss Annie's voice came again. "I heard that," she said. "I didn't even think about the girls. I don't know why I didn't. Actually . . ." Another little silence. "I'll talk to them about it. If there are any girls who want to come and work, I don't see why they shouldn't."

"Maybe they won't want to, really," Mother said. "I'm afraid Marly's different. She's rather a tomboy—"

"Mother, I'm not!"

"You are too," said Joe.

"Just wait and see then!" Marly said.

Miss Annie was laughing over the phone. She had a good big laugh, and Mother had to put the telephone twelve inches from her ear or it would've popped her eardrums. "Tell that girl of yours I learned about those Indians today," she said. "I looked it up in a book in the library. The librarian told me where to find it. The story goes that an Indian squaw was cooking for her husband, see, some sort of porridge Indians ate. I guess we'd call it mush now. Anyway, she didn't want to go clear to the spring for the water and happened to have set a pot near a maple tree where her husband had stuck his spear up, and his bow. So she used the 'tree water' that had dripped into this pot, and her husband said he'd never tasted his mush so good and sweet. So she showed him what she'd cooked it in. And after that they boiled mush in 'sweet tree water' every spring."

"What a nice story," Mother said.

"And that superintendent—honestly, I thought I'd never get out of that office, he was so interested. He used to live on a farm himself. Said he remembered when his grandfather used to drive a team of oxen to pull the flatboat in the bush. It was so deep with mud even horses couldn't make it, he said. He rode on top of the sap tank—"

She went on and on. Everybody in that school seemed to have told Miss Annie a story.

Mother had barely hung up when the phone rang again. And it was Chrissie! She said that Chris was a lot better, and that he was so happy about the sugar crop going right along in spite of everything that it was helping him to get better. To have the children come and help would relieve him even more, she said. "The only thing that worried him was you folks having to work so hard—especially Marly," Chrissie said.

About Annie-Get-Your-Gun she laughed and laughed. She said she could hardly wait to go back and tell Mr. Chris all about it.

The next day the school bus went by as usual. But pretty soon it came back again. Boys *and girls* simply swarmed up the hill! Fritz got them organized, so many to go out with him each time. It seemed like magic how quickly the buckets were emptied and into the storage tanks. Long before noon everybody was back in school again—even Joe and Marly.

"Why didn't you tell me so I could come, too?" Margie wailed when Marly told her the story of Annie and the children and the Indians and everything.

Next day the teacher let her come. It was getting colder and colder, and the wind changed and blew from the north. When it froze that night, only a little bit of sap was in each bucket, so nothing was hurt at all. Little round islands of frozen sap simply waited in the buckets for the next thaw.

It was cold for nearly a week. Mr. Chris wrote his first letter before the next big run began. "I've never heard of anything so fine in all my life, all those children helping out," he wrote. His writing looked a little bit shaky, but all the way down the page it seemed to get stronger and stronger, until he wrote his name big and firm: CHRIS. Then there was a huge postscript, that said, "Marly, it looks like there's been another miracle on Maple Hill."

14 MR. CHRIS GETS A TASTE

The day before Mr. Chris came home from the hospital, Marly found the first spring beauty. The sugaring was over, and she and Joe were helping Fritz pull the buckets. That one flower stood all alone in a patch of sun, one bright pink spot on the brown leaves under a maple tree.

It seemed to be a sign. Carefully she took it up, bringing with it some leaves and soil as Mr. Chris had told her to. She wanted to put it in a flowerpot to stand beside his bed.

Mother and Daddy were waiting when she came home from school on *the day*. The school bus was late, and of course they had to wait for Joe. Marly thought it would never come. But at last they were on the way, Marly carrying her little flowerpot and Mother holding a huge cake on which she had put the words, *Welcome Home, Mr. Chris!*

"Chrissie says there's nothing wrong with his appetite," Mother said.

Chrissie came out onto the porch to welcome them, just as she had done that first day. As they all went up the stairs, she said, laughing, "I tell you, I wasn't one bit sure there for a while whether we'd ever see this day . . ."

Marly stood in the doorway and let the others go in first. Mr. Chris's voice was his own, big and strong from the bed, with his laugh booming out toward her. But he was a huge island of sheets, and his skin looked strangely white.

"Where's my girl?" he asked, and held out his arms. Then she forgot how strange he looked and ran to him. He reached out and took her directly into a hug that didn't smell of Mr. Chris and the earth at all, but of soap and medicine. Yet here he was. But—oh, how awful! She had forgotten all about that little pot. Over the sheets was spilled the earth and leaves and the poor little pink spring beauty.

"Oh, dear!" Mother said. "Marly, you *would* do a thing like that!"

"It's the first spring beauty," she said. "I had it in this pot—"

Mr. Chris sat looking at the brown earth and the tumbled old leaves and picked up the flower by its long thin stem. "It's beautiful, Marly," he said. "I didn't dream you could find one already. I've been wondering how they were coming along this spring."

"There are buds on the hepaticas—just starting," she said. "And there'll be yellow violets by Sunday."

He looked at Chrissie. She was wiping her eyes for some reason and blowing her nose. "I guess I'm home," Mr. Chris said. "I guess it's all starting over, isn't it?"

Then the sheet was taken off and shaken clean and the flower fixed again in its little pot. Everybody talked at once. They were gay with relief and at being together again. Marly stopped being afraid Mr. Chris might break if she touched him or the bed, and sat perched at the foot.

"And now that syrup," Mr. Chris finally said. "Fritz says

he thinks it's pretty good. How about letting me have a taste of it?"

Suddenly everybody was quiet. This was the moment, wasn't it, when they would find out for sure how well or how badly they had done? Mr. Chris *knew*. It was one of the things a man learned gradually, but after forty years of springs and runs and carrying buckets and keeping fires, he knew whether the syrup was right or wasn't.

Marly looked at Daddy, and Daddy sat looking at the floor, twiddling his thumbs.

"I'm afraid it's not like yours, Chris," he said. "Even though we used the thermometer—maybe because we did. See—we didn't want to give your good old customers our syrup and spoil your reputation, so—"

Mr. Chris laughed, but nobody else did. Even Chrissie.

"So," Daddy went on, "we decided we'd keep what we did apart from what you finished before you left. We didn't put any of your labels on our cans."

There was a little silence. Then Mr. Chris cleared his throat and said, "Dale, it's *bound* to be—"

"No. No, it isn't, Chris," Mother said quickly. "You know how we feel. Why, all Dale's ever heard from me is how absolutely perfect your syrup is. I always got that gallon from you at Christmas, marked first-run Chris—and signed with your name. He couldn't feel any different about it."

"That order came from Florida the other day," Fritz said. "From that fellow who always sends the special crate for ten first-run gallons. Like Dale said, we could just tell him how it's been this year."

A little frown was on Mr. Chris's forehead. "What's the matter with it? Did you *burn* it or something?" he asked.

"Heavens, no!" Daddy said. "Why, Chris, we watched it like hawks. Actually, as far as watching goes and getting the sap into the pans as soon as it came in, we did all that."

"We sure did," Fritz said. Joe nodded, and Mother nodded. Marly thought of the long, cold hours and felt a sudden pain in her arm muscles, as if they remembered, too.

"Well, then, let me taste it," said Mr. Chris. "I'm starved for a taste of good syrup after that imitation stuff they served at that hospital. Sort of watered-down mixture they had. Had it on pancakes last Sunday."

"Well, then—" Daddy looked at Fritz.

Fritz started for the door.

"Let *me* get it!" Marly cried. "I know where it is."

"I'll get it," Joe said. "Marly, it's too heavy for a girl to lug that whole gallon can clear upstairs."

"Heavy? *One* gallon heavy? Why, I've carried as much as four gallons clear from that big end tree to the flatboat, and you know it!"

Everybody began to laugh. Daddy said, "Well, I guess I'll have to toss up for this one." He took a nickel from his pocket. "Heads or tails, Marly?"

She hesitated. She tried to think of some special sign that would be sure to make it sure. Suddenly she thought about the foxes and said quickly, "Tails!"

Daddy flipped the nickel up, and it came down and rolled along the floor. It was heads. Joe went with a whoop toward the door.

"Marly, Chris can't taste that syrup out of that gallon tin, can he?" Chrissie asked. "If you'd like to go down to the kitchen and get him a cup and a spoon—"

Marly came back upstairs after Joe, carrying the cup and spoon carefully while he lugged the heavy can. They all stood around while Daddy unscrewed the little lid and poured some syrup carefully into the cup in Marly's hands.

"Now," he said.

"Don't spill *that* on the bed, for goodness' sakes!" Mother said. Marly moved carefully over the floor, holding the cup with both hands.

Mr. Chris reached out and took it from her. They both moved so carefully one would have thought they carried a magic potion like those in the fairy stories—some drink that could make a person grow suddenly tall or suddenly small, like Alice in Wonderland. Maybe some magic liquid that would help Mr. Chris not to be sick any more, but to live forever and forever.

He lifted it close to his face and took a big taste, holding it in his mouth a while, tasting. Then he swallowed, slowly. And then he smiled.

"Joe," he said, "are you *sure* you got what these fellows made? Sure you didn't make a mistake and pick up some of that first-run stuff I finished off myself?"

"No, sir," Joe said seriously. But everybody else was laughing.

"I swear on the Bible I couldn't tell the difference if I tried for ten years," Mr. Chris said. He looked into the cup deeply as if he gazed into a well. "Color—fragrance—*everything!*" he said.

"I guess you must be a mighty good teacher," Daddy said.

Then everybody was talking at once again. How many gallons—what a wonderful crop!—how perfect the sugaring weather had been for days and weeks. There was an article

in a Pittsburgh newspaper that said it was the greatest sugaring year in the whole history of Pennsylvania!

"You see, Marly?" Mr. Chris said, and pulled her onto the bed, beside his pillow. "It's because you came. It must be because you folks came."

Out of the window, over his head, she could see the trees where millions of tiny new buds were beginning. So it would begin over and over, she thought, always and always, the miracles on Maple Hill.